MW01241678

The Life of a Dog and Other Tales

Gary has shared with us some insightful, well-crafted tales of life in the Midwest in the 1950s and '60s. *The Life of a Dog and Other Tales* is a welcome walk down memory lane for many of us who grew up in simpler times. So put your electronic gear in airplane mode, grab a glass of sweet tea, sit back, and enjoy a few tales from a master storyteller.

–GENE P. MARLIN
Acting Director, Illinois State Police (retired)

Gary Totten's *The Life of a Dog and Other Tales* is true life storytelling at its best. Readers will feel both entertained and fulfilled by the stories, and the people in his stories are the genuine article described as only one who lived in the Midwest can do it!

–CARL J. BARGER
Author of *Arkansas Hillbilly: One Man's Memoir of a Blessed Life*

I sometimes laughed and sometimes shed a tear while I read *The Life of a Dog and Other Tales* and thought about the beauty seen in relationships, even those that might not be easy. Yes, there is nostalgia in the stories, but what really makes it a book to savor is that it reminds us of some of the most important aspects of life.

–COLONEL DANNY R. HUNDLEY
United States Marine Corps (Retired)

The Life of a Dog
and Other Tales

The Life of a Dog
and Other Tales

Stories from the
Rural Heartland

Gary Totten

BLACKBERRY PUBLISHING
PO Box 245
Noble, Illinois 62868

The Life of a Dog and Other Tales:
Stories from the Rural Heartland
Gary Totten

ISBN: 978-0-9988656-0-7 (print)
LCCN: 2017905792

EDITING by Melanie Mulhall, Dragonheart
(*www.DragonheartWritingandEditing.com*)
BOOK DESIGN by Bob Schram, Bookends Design
(*www.BookendsDesign.com*)

Published by Blackberry Publishing
PO Box 245
Noble, Illinois 62868

CONTENTS

1

Joe's Tonsorial Emporium

 THOSE WHO KNEW HIM WELL and liked him thought him a genius. Those who knew him well and didn't like him thought him eccentric at best and a bizarre oddity at worst.

Even with the passing of forty years since those days, I still haven't made up my mind about him. Was he an energetic intellectual, never quite able to channel his abilities in the right direction, or was he just a small-town character plagued by obsessive-compulsive tendencies? Whatever he was, he was interesting.

I met Joe in 1965. I had graduated from high school in the spring and was a freshman at the local junior college, along with most of my high school friends. Life was mostly going to school, hunting, fishing, and searching for girls in and around my small southeastern Illinois town.

It actually seemed like just a continuation of high school—same town, same people, same things to do—just a different building for school with a new set of teachers.

One of my friends first mentioned that a new barber had opened up in town on East Main, and he had a reputation for doing an excellent job. In fact, he was so exacting and thorough in his work that it took him a full hour to do one haircut. I was at an age when I thought there was a direct relationship between the quality of one's haircut and the quality of one's love life, and my friend said that a haircut at Joe's was an experience to be remembered. Since I had no loyalty to anyone else, I decided to enhance my romantic chances at the Dog 'n Suds Drive In with a trip to Joe's.

In those days, no one had ever heard of making an appointment to get a haircut, at least not in my hometown. You went on Saturday, waited for up to two hours for those ahead of you to be cut, and read the same issue of *Outdoor Life or Prairie Farmer* that you had read last time while listening to casual talk about the weather and counting the number of hats on the coatrack that advertised seed corn. The only relief from this necessary but trying wait was perhaps dropping a dime in the pop machine in return for a Nehi grape pop.

Joe made appointments. You could walk in and wait, or you could call and prearrange a convenient time and save yourself another update on how far along the soy beans were up by Stringtown or down by Bone Gap. You could forego the bimonthly jail sentence that constituted the long wait and plan instead to wash your car or install speakers in the backseat to assist in wooing some dolly to a frenzied romantic state on Saturday night. And you could make an appointment anytime! That's right, anytime. Whether you wanted to stop by at 7:00 a.m. or 8:30 p.m., Joe was flexible. What if you had a date and wanted a haircut after you took Charlotte home at midnight? No problem. Joe's schedule could conform to yours. Groovy, as we said in those days.

The only exterior feature that physically distinguished Joe's barbershop from any other ordinary edifice for such purposes in any other ordinary little town was his sign, Joe's Tonsorial Emporium.

Upon entering the front door, even the most preoccupied customer could tell that this was no ordinary barbershop. It was neat, organized, spotless, and exact. Shelves containing rows of hair tonic lined the far wall. Each row of bottles, lined up front to back, was in perfect alignment. The space between each bottle of Lucky Tiger and each row of Fitch's Hair Tonic was consistent. The rows, shelves, and quantities—enough for all the male heads in two small towns—were balanced with each other. No dust was permitted.

The wall along the front of the room that framed the big picture window was lined with chairs for those waiting for their appointed hour and those who came to watch. Tables between the chairs contained neatly arranged piles of magazines, stacked in chronological order by month and year. The latter observation is somewhat theoretical because no one ever conjured up the courage to go in more than a magazine or two deep. To do so would be to risk the disruption of their strict order, with sides and corners appearing uniform from any angle of view. To significantly disturb such order would somehow be an invasion of Joe's privacy or at least result in his nervous glance in your direction.

The wall directly across from the front contained the barber chair, which was ordinary looking except for a rotating stool that was welded to a moveable sleeve at a point just above the base. This unique arrangement allowed Joe to sit down while practicing his trade. The stool swiveled and was capable of swinging from one side of the chair to the other so quickly that its occupant appeared almost a blur as he pivoted from left to right, studying an approach to some unruly patch of hair. He would rest most of his weight on the stool with one leg touching the floor to provide a source of propulsion for his dynamic moves, creating a motion-packed spectacle as he flew about, intensely focused on his work.

The stool was evidently required because of a bad leg. Joe had been in an auto accident many years before and, according to him, his leg now contained several pounds of metal and wire. Long periods of standing irritated it.

His taller than average, thin, wiry frame would appear to lift the leg a little stiffly as he walked, but movement was still in a hurried, agile manner. His nervous and purposeful gait created a noisy presence because keys and pocket change rattled in their constant rearrangement.

At the time, Joe was probably no older than forty. He had grown up in a neighboring town and served in the Navy during the Korean War. His hair was thinning on top and looked as though it might have been sandy or reddish in color during his younger years, but it had now turned darker and begun to gray. He had been married once and had a grown son, somewhere, whom he spoke of occasionally.

It was rumored that Joe had been pressured to leave a nearby town for falsifying IDs for those not quite old enough to legally purchase alcohol and for other shady activities. Although I never knew that for sure, I did know that he had many entrepreneurial interests, including making a trip to Missouri every summer to purchase fireworks to sell under the table, or under the chair in this case. He was an avid coin collector and frequently described some trade or transaction that improved his position.

Once you had gained his confidence as a regular customer, especially if you had a late appointment when the emporium was empty, he would unexpectedly disappear into his back room and reappear with a cigar box containing assorted novelty condoms. The items, which were for sale individually or in multi-packets, were of various colors, styles, and characteristics, which he would note with a boyish, mischievous air. These definitely were not of the gas station variety, known to leave their circular imprint in one's billfold after carrying the same one for six months. It is likely that Joe had several other enterprising sidelines that were unknown to me.

Joe had a great many hobbies and interests, and one was increasing his vocabulary. His patrons were occasionally challenged, perhaps right in the middle of the delicate and tense process of getting their sideburns squared off, with a new word that had caught Joe's eye. "Do you know the meaning of the word 'lycanthropy'?" he would ask. Then he'd amuse himself for a few moments, displaying a discreet and knowing smile, while you prepared your best guess. All the while, he toyed with your lack of knowledge and built suspense until he at last declared the meaning of the word. His smile transformed into chuckles in much the same way I imagine the chairman of the board at General Motors might have announced the design for the new '66 models.

Joe was always quick to offer customers coffee as they walked in the door. If the offer was accepted, he would carefully tear off a paper towel precisely at the perforations, place a plastic cup holder on the towel, place a disposable coffee cup in the holder, carefully pour in the hot beverage to just the right level, and bring it, towel and all, to the customer's chair. He monitored the customer's progress in consuming the coffee and when finished, the cup and towel were quickly disposed of.

Using the bathroom at Joe's was a unique experience. He explained that his profession was licensed and that his facility was subject to unannounced and random inspections by the state. The patron was therefore advised that cleanliness was of utmost concern. For example, before exiting the bathroom, one was required to procure a paper towel from the roll placed there, dry and polish the metal faucet handles, and wipe clean the interior of the sink. Of course, these instructions were not posted, but verbally provided when someone asked to use the bathroom.

The haircut itself was a wealth of tradition and procedure. After getting the new customer seated in the chair, Joe paced around him, mentally forming a plan of attack. Then he conducted his first haircut interview. "Now, some individuals like variety from haircut to haircut or like something a little different from time to time, and other individuals pretty much like the same thing each haircut. Which type of individual are you?"

As he spoke those last words, he zoomed in on the customer's face with the concentrated attention of one preparing for brain surgery and intently awaited a response.

"Well, Joe, I pretty much like it the same way each time," a customer usually replied.

That was followed by a formal declaration from Joe. "Well then, I'll make up a card on you."

Joe kept cards on all his regular customers.

"First, let's start with the burns. Now, do you generally like your sideburns short, medium, or long in length?" Once the issue of the burns had been resolved and recorded, he moved quickly to hair length. "Now, on the sides, do you keep the length short, medium, or long?" These questions were posed in a most serious manner, and the response was awaited in equally solemn silence.

And so it went as Joe entered the pertinent information on a three-by-five note card. All details were documented, with room for individual client idiosyncrasies. At the conclusion of the day, Joe stamped the date on the back of the card for future reference. On subsequent appointments, the customer's card was pulled and reviewed before the work was begun.

His recordkeeping was a matter of some pride for him, and my friends and I were constantly putting him to the test. "Joe, on what date did I get a haircut before Christmas last year?" The correct answer would be retorted in a split second. "Joe, how many haircuts did I get the first six months last year?" Again, Joe had this vital information readily available, and it was happily and proudly provided.

The intensity and excitement built as the haircut progressed, much to the glee of the observers. Great care was taken to match the length of the sideburns. Such care required that Joe lower himself to a position very close to and in front of the customer's face, which was somewhat disturbing to the first-timer. Without moving his head, Joe's eyes darted intently from one sideburn to the other to ascertain each burn's relationship to the other until a decision resulted in a slight adjustment to one or the other.

The final throes of the haircut could only be likened to a shark's feeding frenzy. The tension and concentration were increasingly visible on his face and in his actions. Faster and faster, he spun around the draped customer on his pivoting stool, cutting a tiny bit here or there, first clearing his throat, then nervously brushing off a speck of hair on his or the customer's shirt as if he were Michelangelo putting the last brush strokes on the ceiling of the Sistine Chapel. In a flurry of quick, jumpy movements, it appeared that each arm and leg flew in a circle, the way a schoolyard merry-go-round spins around its center. In the middle of this excitement, he would stop abruptly, turn from the customer, face the mirror, quickly comb his own hair, and immediately return his attention to the matter at hand.

Finally, just when the customer was about to be stricken with the urge to laugh hysterically and run screaming into the street, it would be over. Over, that is, except for the vacuum cleaner. A small vacuum cleaner was mounted from the ceiling above the chair. Once the sheet was removed from the chair's occupant, the vacuum was activated and the customer was thoroughly cleaned from the waist up. This operation began with the front and sides. Then, with great speed and strength, as if free-ing an object lodged in the throat, the customer was thrust forward in the seat to make his back accessible. But Joe did not stop there. He then unbuttoned the customer's shirt about halfway down and plunged the nozzle down it to the waist, both front and back.

Next, with shirt still opened, the customer was given a very large hand mirror and asked to study his hair. Was it okay in back? Were the burns just right? For Joe, this moment was more than a haircut critique. He was a plastic surgeon who had just completed a delicate and complex procedure, and the medical school director was studying the results. Or he was a famous sculptor who had just un-veiled a great work and waited anxiously for comments.

Positive remarks were followed by several thank-yous, first gratefully audible and then in a series almost under his breath.

During the two or three years that I visited the emporium regularly, several new friends were treated—or should I say exposed—to a visit to Joe's. The unsuspecting friend would schedule an appointment and several of us would happen along for a cup of coffee to watch. The half-amused, half-uneasy expression on their faces with Joe twirling around them was not only a show on a rainy Saturday afternoon, it was the topic of many funny stories and jokes for years afterward.

But those weren't the only stories produced by the events at Joe's Tonsorial Emporium. There were many others. One in particular involved his Boy Friday. At some point, Joe concluded that his business had progressed to the point that he needed to retain an employee to do odd jobs around the shop. He always referred to his workers as Friday, and he had many, one at a time. It was a strong-willed boy who could last a week in Joe's employment. Many terminated the relationship during the first day.

The emporium was sparsely occupied one afternoon when I was in the barber chair. A new Friday with bushy red hair was being dispatched here and there, under extremely close supervision. It was time to fill some small bottles with a liquid hair product from a large container.

"Friday, go to the back room and get the small wooden stool," Joe instructed.

Friday complied at once.

"Now, set the stool in the center of the floor here, placing each leg on a different square tile in the pattern of tiles on the floor."

Friday did as he was asked.

"Good. Now tear off a paper towel and lay it across the top of the stool. Then place an empty bottle on the center of the paper towel and place that funnel in the bottle."

Friday complied, though I could tell from the look on his face that he was clueless about the reasons for what he was being asked to do.

"Fine," Joe said, nodding in approval. "Now, you are going to pour the liquid from the large container into the smaller bottle just until it reaches the neck of the bottle. I'm going to tell you three times how I want you to pour. Slow and easy. Slow and easy. Slow and easy. Now, go ahead."

Friday's eyes had become larger as the instructions progressed, and his face became fearful and expectant. He probably wished that he was safely back home with his mother. All eyes were on Friday as he lifted the container. The liquid gushed forward as he raised the bottom, quickly filling the smaller bottle, then the funnel. Like a waterfall caused by spring runoff, it then spilled over the funnel to the stool and onto the floor.

The fearful look on the boy's face was replaced with one of horror. All eyes turned to Joe, including Friday's. Joe's first reaction was to be physically taken aback by this great catastrophe that had befallen his neat, organized life and had ruined the inner sanctum of his tidy world. He rushed to the disaster site while launching a loud and highly charged invective, fraught with obscenities.

Poor Friday, frozen in his tracks, could only watch as Joe proceeded to clean the mess. I don't recall ever seeing

that particular Friday again, although I do recall that a
later Friday was finally employed who could see the humor
in it all and stayed for quite some time.

Eventually, I left town for the last years of college, and
my visits to Joe became less frequent. They ended completely when I graduated and moved even farther away.

Several years later, Joe gained financial independence
and left his profession. During his term with the Navy, he
had been exposed to asbestos while working in a shipyard.
He had finally been awarded a large settlement from the
government after many years of effort on his part to gain
one. Although he had complained about asbestos-related
lung problems, asbestos was just something we put around
hot pipes and used for attic insulation in those days. Joe was
the only person I knew who thought it posed any danger.

After closing the emporium doors for the last time, Joe
purchased a nice home in a good residential area. As could
be expected, his unique approach to his affairs continued
to demonstrate his quirkiness. Joe had a conflict with one
of his neighbors about the neighbor's cat because, Joe complained, the feline lacked respect for the boundaries of his
lawn. The conflict escalated and eventually led to the filing
of a court case, as well as the unexpected late night demise
of the cat. To clarify, the death was unexpected by the cat
and its owner, but not by Joe.

Later adventures included Joe's run for mayor, during
which he launched a vigorous and colorful campaign. Although Joe's intense and dedicated style might have resulted in great initiatives and undertakings, the small voter

response in his favor seemed to indicate that the community was not quite ready for Joe's brand of leadership.

Years later, I ran into Joe one last time at an American Legion event. He recognized me immediately, and we reminisced for a while about his many years at the emporium, recalling the names of many of his former customers and their current whereabouts.

Since my days at the emporium, I have had hundreds of haircuts provided by at least two dozen barbers with a wide variety of approaches and results, some good and some not. None have reached the level of tonsorial standards, customer service, pride of work, and downright fun provided by Joe's Tonsorial Emporium. Only a very few have offered coffee, and not a single one has sold firecrackers and condoms. And none have plunged a vacuum cleaner hose down the inside of my shirt.

2

The Great Levitation

MOST OF US HAVE ONE OR TWO very odd or unusual happenings in our life, perhaps a string of hard-to-believe coincidences or a witnessing of some borderline paranormal or supernatural event. Although I don't know anyone who has claimed to have been abducted by aliens and subsequently returned to Earth claiming they were subjected to experiments using chickens, I have met people I respect who have related some pretty weird stories.

I've led a common life myself, which is just fine and dandy with me. There is a lot to be said for the ordinary—enjoying and appreciating family and friends, watching a thunderstorm from the front porch, the smell of coffee and bacon early in the morning, a good night's sleep after a hard day's work—that leaves me with a feeling of accomplishment. But one event floats to the top for me as a strange set of circumstances and actions.

It was the summer of 1965. I had graduated from high school in May and was lucky enough to find a summer job to help with college expenses starting in the fall. My friend Steve Tice (hereinafter referred to as Tice) and I spent our spare time bass fishing and running around in his mother's blue and white 1963 Chevrolet Bel Air. While some of our friends had their own cars, neither of us could afford that. We were perfectly content and pleased that his trusting mother, Virginia, would loan us hers. She might not have been so generous if she had known that Tice was a little rough on it. In his defense, some fishing holes were at the end of muddy roads with ruts so deep that they would hold water even in a dry August.

One hot, sticky day in late June, Tice and I were tooling around in his mom's car. Many cars didn't have air conditioning in those days, but the Chevy did, and it was so hot out that we had to run the air conditioner at full blast to keep cool. As was our custom, much of our cruising was done out of town, exploring country roads or driving out to the beach at the lake to see who was hanging out there. Normally, such drives concluded at the White Spot, the place to go for ice cream long before the Dairy Queen came to town.

But on this day, we decided to stop at the Lakeside Grocery. This country store was located on the state highway north of town and at the edge of Vernor Lake, one of the town's water supply lakes. Although Vernor Lake was its formal name, everyone in the county called it the rez, short for reservoir. The store had a small gravel parking area in front that was accessed by pulling directly off the highway.

Like most country stores in the county, it was family owned and staffed by various family members. The store at the rez was owned by Roy and Lucy Fehrenbacher, who by the mid-sixties rarely worked at the counter because they were blessed with a large number of kids who were old enough to manage the business during the day. Jody, Pat, and Mary could be found working there on most days, either alone or as a group. The boys never seemed to be there, perhaps because they preferred to be outside and their parents let them off the hook. Since the family also lived in the rooms connected to the store, it was easy for anyone working to come and go into the residence portion of the edifice. In fact, there wasn't even a door separating the living quarters from the store.

Having grown up in a house on the lake, Tice knew the Fehrenbachers well. His family hadn't moved into town until the previous year, and he now lived but a block from my family's house. But for all the years before that, he had lived out at the lake. We had many friends about our age who also lived around or near the lake and had spent many summer days there fishing, swimming, or just hanging out. The store was the primary focus for neighbors and a convenient place to loiter and visit, where a small purchase of a bottle of Royal Crown Cola might entitle the customer to loafing rights for an hour.

Mary and Pat Fehrenbacher were twins, and a more friendly and easygoing pair you could not find. These jolly, heavyset girls laughed easily at our dumb jokes and were a little gullible when it came to some of our farfetched tales. With Jody, however, the twinkle in her eye and big smile let us know that she received our stories with a grain of salt.

Tice and Roy Fehrenbacher had been sparking off of each other like two live wires for years. Roy's serious and businesslike nature was in conflict with Tice's mischievous nature, which he imposed on Roy in a series of witty and risky confrontations. Years earlier, Roy had driven Tice from the store, exclaiming, "You belong in an institution!"

On this day, Tice and I had pulled into the hot, dusty parking lot and parked close to the front door, the sole vehicle in sight. As it happened, Pat and Mary were working. We each got a bottle of RC Cola, always ice-cold from the old cooler, and proceeded to enjoy the good company of the twins.

To this day, I miss the first cold swig of pop from a glass bottle. Since the advent of aluminum cans and plastic containers, a cold drink on a hot day just has not been the same, much like drinking coffee from a Styrofoam cup lacks the enjoyment offered from drinking coffee from a nice porcelain mug.

Our visiting concluded and bottles empty, we headed out the door into the sweltering heat. Tice jumped into the driver's seat, quickly started the engine, and turned the fan up to high. We left the doors open a couple of minutes to blow the hot air to the outside, but once the inside started to cool off and we had closed the doors, the discussion turned to cherry bombs.

Most fireworks were illegal in Illinois then, just as they are now, but they were always available if you knew the right people. If not, a drive to Missouri, where they were legal, was possible and common for the area.

Everything about cherry bombs was cool. About the size of a quarter, they were round and red with a green fuse. When they exploded, they made a terrific loud boom that was not a low-pitched sonic-type boom, but a shrill, forceful, deafening boom that would make dogs a quarter mile away jump to their feet and bark. They could even be lit and thrown in a pond, where they would explode underwater, causing small bluegill to float paralyzed to the surface, an occurrence I had personally witnessed.

Being only days away from the Fourth of July, Tice happened to have some cherry bombs in his possession and present in a paper bag on the front seat. "Hey, let's light one of these up and scare the Fehrenbacher twins," he said, smiling wryly. "We can throw one right in front of the front door and drive off!"

He pushed in the cigarette lighter, whipped one out of the bag, waited until the light was glowing red, and touched the lighter to the fuse.

In those days, it was manly to hold the cherry bomb in one's fingers for a second or two before actually throwing it. Why waste time watching a bomb fizz and smoke around on the ground when you could display bravery, cunning, and agility all in one tense and expectant moment. In a quick and fluid movement, my confident buddy jerked his cherry bomb laden hand to the window at the last possible instant. This action resulted in a sharp snapping sound as his class ring smacked against the window glass.

The window was closed! The smoking cherry bomb immediately dropped to the seat between his legs.

What happened next happened in slow motion, just like in the movies, with exaggerated movements and the sound of loud, low-pitched, slow-speaking human voices. As his wide-eyed head turned in my direction, Tice screamed, "Je . . . sus Chri . . . st! Lets . . . get . . . out . . . of heerree!"

At the same moment those words were traveling through space to my ears, his tall, lanky frame levitated from the seat of the '63 Bel Air, still in slow motion, with no help whatsoever from his appendages. I know his legs were not involved in the movement because they, too, were ascending while remaining perpendicular to the seat. Once his body was completely elevated, he floated unassisted to a position immediately above me. As he descended onto my lap, four hands were grabbing madly for the door handle in a hopeless and pitiful attempt to escape.

Two extremes of sound followed. First, there was a loud bang to accompany what must have been a magnum cherry bomb, which had maintained its location on the driver's side seat during the levitation experience. Next, a sound erupted that I had not heard before nor have heard since, an extremely high-pitched and continuous *eeee*. I looked toward the highway and observed traffic going by, making no audible sound whatsoever. It was as if my hearing had been completely switched off and replaced by a thousand pieces of chalk screeching on a blackboard.

The event was over. Tice was sitting in my lap as I opened the car door, and we crawled out back into the oven-like heat. We tried to talk. Moving lips could be seen, but only faint words could be heard.

Gradually, our hearing improved, but not for many hours. I have no idea if the blast was heard inside the store or if there were any witnesses to the great levitation. We were preoccupied with thinking up a story that would explain the burnt hole in the seat of the '63 Chevy Bel Air.

We couldn't tell the truth. Tice's mother would have pronounced us liars, not because she couldn't imagine Tice pitching cherry bombs and forgetting to roll down the car window, but because no one in those parts believed in levitation. Nope, we needed a plausible explanation, something like a well-placed lightning strike or an errant raccoon with a cigar.

It took us the rest of the day to craft a story we thought she might swallow.

3

The Duffel Bag Kid

 IT MUST HAVE BEEN THE SAME KIND of dark, snowy morning that inspired John Greenleaf Whittier to write "Snow-Bound" over a hundred years ago in which he began:

The sun that brief December day
Rose cheerless over hills of gray,
And, darkly circled, gave at noon,
A sadder light than waning moon.

Fort Lewis, Washington, a US Army military base, lies a few miles southwest of Tacoma, Washington, just north of the tiny town of Roy, and it is the home of the Nisqually Indian Tribe. Many would describe the countryside as beautiful on a clear day. Sunlight bounces off the rocky hills, covered with pine trees, an inspiring example of the

Pacific Northwest. I can say with certainty, however, that it was a cold, wet, miserable place for a young fellow to be confined during the winter of 1968-69. It was also a setting where young men, nervous about their future during the height of the Viet Nam War, experienced what it was like to be oriented into military life, with all its traditions, interactions, discomforts, and humor. As Steve "Pooh" Sinkler said in the thick of it, "Boys, I've seen hard times and I've seen bad times, but these are hard, bad times!"

As a student at Eastern Illinois University during the late sixties, I was hoping to graduate in the spring of 1969. Having only lived with my parents prior to college, I was not very worldly. I was pretty conservative and focused mostly on classes and homework. Four friends and I had rented rooms in off-campus housing. An older couple, Mom and Pop as we called them, owned a large home on Tenth Street. They lived on the main floor. The students had a bathroom and bedrooms upstairs and a kitchen and rumpus room in the basement. It was several blocks to the campus, but it was an enjoyable walk past older homes on tree-lined sidewalks.

The military draft was alive and well in those days, and the Viet Nam War was surging on. If you were a healthy male college student, as I was at the time, the draft was always in the back of your mind. If you watched the six o'clock news, the draft was pushed to the front of your mind like a noisy bulldozer moaning and clanking as it pushed a heavy pile of bricks up to your feet, with the heat and dust filling your senses. In your billfold was a draft card from your local county draft board declaring that your 4a (full-time college student) draft status was a hungry piranha fish that was gnawing its way through the leather compartments and would reach your tender young buttocks within two weeks of your college graduation.

Then, just as it is today, there were many different opinions and emotions regarding the American effort in a country halfway across the world that very few had heard of before the war. It wasn't a place we studied in geography. It took me a while to even find it on the globe we had on the desk upstairs.

A few college students were enthusiastic, I suppose, for the day when their deferment status would end and they would take their turn to better the world by stopping the spread of communism. But most of us were confused about what the war meant to us personally and what it meant for the country. Like me, most had fathers who had served during World War II and grandfathers who had served in World War I. And like me, most had resigned themselves to the fact that they, too, would serve and do their best just like the last two generations, regardless of the war's lack of popularity and their personal opinions. I knew of no one from my area giving serious consideration to moving to Canada to avoid the draft, but of course, that was not uncommon in some areas.

On some days the war, or "conflict," to be politically correct, seemed perfectly logical and necessary to me. And to pay our dues, to be patriotic, and to enter manhood under upright, traditional circumstances, military service was something that all young men from all generations had to do. Besides, it was necessary if you wanted to become a member of the American Legion in my hometown, and membership in the American Legion enabled you to stop by the post for a beer and swap stories after a warm Saturday of catching bluegill out at the lake.

But on other days, the effort did not seem as logical. The news was filled with demonstrators and war protestors, some of whom made good points. And once, as I walked by the campus union, I saw a large piece of plywood on which was painted an acerbic question: What worse fate than to be killed on a day when the six o'clock news reports that casualties were light?

During my junior year, military discussions turned toward the Army National Guard. Growing up in a rural area of southern Illinois, I was aware of National Guard units around the Midwest and familiar with some men, especially farmers, who had been joining since the Korean conflict.

Although this was a six-year commitment, it was a way to fulfill the military obligation. Eventually, most of my hometown friends who had gone to college decided to consider it. It soon became clear, though, that hundreds of others had already had the same thought and were wearing ruts in the armory sidewalks, trying to sign up. It seemed that all National Guard units in the country had very long waiting lists comprised of those interested in joining, and those first on the list had been waiting for close to two years. Realizing that this was a long shot, several of us added our names to a couple of lists, knowing that vacancies would not occur prior to graduation and that in all likelihood, we would soon be at the medical clearing house in St. Louis being asked to drop our drawers and bend over, at the same time kissing the aforementioned buttocks good-bye.

As fate would have it, a decision was made that the Effingham National Guard unit would change its mission and double in size, becoming a full-fledged infantry company. It would recruit a large number of new troops in a short period of time. When this happened, I was halfway through the fall quarter of my senior year and fully believed that I would be drafted into the army by mid-June of 1969. Rumors soon began circulating among my circle of friends that the waiting list for this particular National Guard unit was getting shorter, prompting even more young men to get their names on the list, just in case. Soon, people I actually knew well were being contacted to come in and sign the paperwork if they were still interested. Finally, sometime in October, I was called in for my physical and was told to report on November 4 to be sworn in.

I spoke to all of my college instructors, and in each case, I was allowed to either take a final exam early for the course or accept the grade average I currently had. Either they were being kind or they were just being patriotic.

I received orders to report for duty at a small airport in Mattoon on November 19. Then I would travel to Ft. Lewis, Washington, for eight weeks of basic training, to be followed by nine weeks of advanced infantry training. These weeks would be preceded by up to two weeks at the base reception center. I was informed by the guard unit to bring only one set of clothes apart from those I was wearing, along with two items issued by the home unit, an olive drab military duffel bag with my name and serial number stenciled on it and an army field jacket of the same hue.

It was a cold, sunny day when I arrived at the small airport in Mattoon along with a fellow from Effingham named Steve Sinkler. We were flown to St. Louis Lambert International Airport for the flight to Seattle. Having not flown before, I was pretty impressed. This was back in the days when onboard meals were served with cloth napkins and small but real silverware. This was to be my last kind treatment before being thrust into the rugged and indifferent melting pot of the army.

A charter bus of some sort was waiting at the Seattle airport to transport me, Steve, and men arriving from other destinations to the base. After a ninety-minute ride to the fort, I gathered up my duffel bag containing my spanking new field jacket and entered an unfriendly world. An army drill sergeant was present outside the bus screaming instructions. He lined up the lost and bewildered souls into our first formation and marched us to the reception center barracks. It must have been an amusing sight as this mismatched bunch of humanity, some with shoulder-length hair, tried for the first time to master the "your left, your left, your left, right, left" cadence.

Although I had heard horror stories about harassment at army reception centers, no harassment was specifically directed towards me. Mostly it was a matter of waiting in long lines to get another assembly-line physical, picking up the standard army issue clothing, and getting vaccinations.

The person in charge of issuing the two pairs of combat boots asked me what size I wore and then issued me boots of a bigger size, which I pointed out to him after checking the size imprinted on them. He gave me a dirty look and said they would fit fine, a prediction that was later discredited by many blisters.

Next, it was time for the famous army haircut. The haircut was an amazing transformation in many cases because of the shoulder-length hippie hair common in those days. It was funny to see a cut in progress, taking the recipient from long locks to hair so short that it couldn't even be grasped between the thumb and index finger. In the following weeks, a haircut was administered once a week as a special treat on Friday.

Once clothing was issued, all personal items were boxed up and mailed home. This included all civilian clothing. If it wasn't issued by the army, you didn't need it. Even rings, family pictures, glasses, and toothbrushes were now contraband. In other words, all you had left that you had arrived with was your naked body, and even that was shaved on top.

The army required that everyone be identical in all possessions except for the name on your uniform and the serial number on your dog tags. This was the beginning of a big problem for me.

While going through the reception center, all of us were issued an army duffel bag and a field jacket. Since I had already been issued these two items, I now had doubles. At first I thought it humorous that the government could not decide how to keep track of its issued items. But when I arrived at my permanent barracks for training, I realized the seriousness of the duplication.

I had managed to avoid being singled out at the reception center, learning through observation that those becoming a target of embarrassing ridicule had opened their mouths with optional comments, taken actions that focused attention on them, or stood out in some manner, even if through no fault of their own. The likelihood of sailing smoothly through any situation in basic training required you to become a wallflower and blend in to the extent that you went unnoticed and appeared as only a common blob of the olive drab color that was everywhere.

This was a technique that I was learning to develop and hone to a fine point. If I caught myself standing alone, for example, I gravitated toward the nearest group of olive drab blobs with intentional subtlety, whether I knew those blobs or not, thereby making myself invisible.

My friend Pooh was not so lucky. Steve "Pooh" Sinkler, my traveling companion from Effingham, Illinois, and I had a couple of short conversations at the armory building, and flying to Seattle together had given us ample time to speculate on what was ahead. I learned that his nickname, a name that stuck as he grew up, sprang from a disgusting event in his childhood. Pooh was a friendly, likable, witty, outgoing fellow who loved to talk, tell stories, and joke around. Although these qualities were all great in a social situation, and I'm sure have since carried him far in life, they were not conducive to blending in.

Although you could converse while waiting in boring lines at the reception center, such communication had to be done with great care. Drill sergeants were everywhere, waiting for the chance to teach and instill the concrete principles of authority and chain of command necessary for any successful military activity. In other words, no order could ever be challenged under any circumstances, no matter how illogical or unfair it might seem.

One day, Pooh was a couple of spaces in line ahead of me and was caught talking by a tough looking, physically fit drill sergeant. After a severe close-up, face-to-face tongue-lashing, Pooh was pointedly asked, "Son, do you like to talk?"

"Yes, Sergeant. I mean, no, Sergeant," replied the wide-eyed Pooh.

"Well, which is it, you piece of crap dud?"

"I'll be quiet, Sergeant," Pooh said, trying to find the right words to appease this fellow who looked like he could find a way to beat you to death with only the use of his glare.

"I'll tell you what, son, I want you to stand here and put your nose on this post."

Pooh complied at once.

"Now, repeat after me, 'Post, I will do what the drill sergeant tells me.' Got it?"

Pooh again assured compliance.

"Now, you stupid piece of crap dud, stand there and keep repeating that loud enough for me to hear you from anywhere in this building, and don't stop until I tell you to. Understood?"

"Yes, Sergeant!" was the response.

Of course, this encounter not only drew a lot of attention, but also served as a reminder to the others in the queue, who were careful only to watch out of the corners of their eyes, lest attention be drawn to them.

I passed Pooh in line at his post and moved slowly forward, his voice becoming more distant the farther I was from him. As his mouth began to tire, the words began to involuntarily reorder themselves. "Post, I will drill what the do Sergeant tells me. Post, I will do. Post, I will drill. Post, I will do what the drill sergeant tells me. Post, . . ."

After rounding the next corner, I could no longer see or hear his voice, and I wondered what would become of him. Regardless, I was glad to be a green blob that was farther away from him.

Our barracks had been quickly built as temporary training structures for World War II soldiers in the early 1940s, some twenty-six years before my arrival. They were built row after row on long streets, and they all looked the same. Each barrack consisted of two floors lined with long vertical windows on each side. Rows of bunk beds lined each wall with an open walkway down the middle so a frisky drill sergeant could move quickly through all the bunks. And each barrack housed a platoon consisting of between forty and fifty men. A barrack had one large bathroom at the end of the first floor. This area consisted of a long row of sinks, two long rows of open toilets, and one shower room. Of course, there was no privacy, and any notions of such were soon forgotten. Bodily functions were never carried out alone unless they occurred between midnight and 4:00 a.m., which was when most of the sleeping was done. Each barrack also had a furnace room accessible through an outside door. Coal was used to heat the edifice, and troops took turns shoveling coal into the stove, day and night in cold weather.

Each group of barracks contained a mess hall, a day room, and a company street. The day room was intended as a common area where soldiers could relax and enjoy time off, although there never really was any time off. It was just an empty room with scant, grungy furniture. The company street was where each day formally began and ended. All formations happened there, and it was the scene of many cadre training speeches, harassment, inspections, and instructions.

The mess hall, a one-story building, was as noisy and busy a place as the day room was empty and silent. If any pause in the long days existed during which you could be alone with your thoughts, it was while waiting in line outside the mess hall doors. There, a person could stand silently at parade rest, arms behind him and hands touching at the waist. He would inch slowly forward, wondering how he came to be there in the first place.

Mess halls were primarily for the dark meals—breakfast before dawn and the evening meal after dark. Lunches were normally brought to the training area, whether that be a gun range or outdoor class setting, since all training was outside. Noon meals were consumed standing up, but for the other meals, troops were allowed the great luxury of sitting down.

No one who has been in the military can forget the sights, sounds, and smells of the mess hall. Upon approaching, there was no distinct smell of food. Displacing the smell of food was the strong smell of industrial detergent, as if you had plunged your face into a box of Tide. Mixed with this pungent smell was the odor of garbage from the last meal, which flowed from repositories behind the mess hall. Upon entering the door, a blast of heat hit your cold face along with the sounds of the steady roar and commotion of people moving, pots and pans clanging, and the strains of whatever very loud music the cooks had playing.

Even though what looked like enough food was flung on the trays as troops filed by the serving line, most troops were hungry most of the time. No talking was allowed during meals, and drill sergeants patrolled the tables looking for those who were eating too slowly. The mess hall could only seat a portion of the company at one time, so soldiers were encouraged to get through the line and eat quickly. You learned how to eat in five minutes and still enjoy it.

Mess hall time was an ideal opportunity for the sergeants to isolate and harass anyone who had become familiar to them through some earlier grievous infraction. An individual would be located and verbally pounced upon until departing the room.

A common mealtime instruction at Ft. Lewis was to put your face down in your plate, suck, and not come up until everything was gone. During one particular evening meal, an example of poor judgement in blending in was highlighted when a skinny troop from somewhere like Kansas or Nebraska was going through the chow line, where cooks spooned food onto the trays of passing troops. This particular fellow noticed that someone in line before him had been the recipient of a somewhat larger portion than he had just received and meekly asked for more.

The cook's stoic face immediately turned to anger. *"What?"*

The poor soldier instantly realized his mistake and did not respond, no doubt hoping he was still in his bunk and just having a nightmare.

"What did you say, idiot?" the cook asked again.

And again, no response was offered.

At that point, the cook beckoned a drill sergeant to the serving line, which had come to a standstill. The cook nodded toward the skinny young man and said, "This guy thinks he needs more food!"

"Well," said the drill sergeant, "he is awful skinny. Let's fill up this runt. How much do you reckon that tray will hold? Fill it up and let's see."

With that, the cook started piling up food on the tray and didn't stop until it was falling off the sides.

"Now, sit your skinny ass down over here, and you better eat every bit of that," the drill sergeant ordered.

No doubt the poor fellow was hoping the sergeant would soon be distracted by some other hideous breach of conduct, but that didn't happen. After the troop was done eating, he was marched outside the mess hall and ordered to run up and down the company street, all the while being encouraged, in a most convincing manner, to run faster. Finally, he could hold it down no longer and lost his lunch. After being chided for wasting good government rations, the sorry fellow was allowed to return to the barracks.

As the weeks crept by, everyone seemed to eventually take his turn at being singled out for some atrocity. Sometimes the color of their hair or their unusual last name was ridiculed. Maybe it was a loose thread found on the sleeve of a field jacket or the sleeve of their itchy long wool underwear slightly making its appearance from under the outer sleeve of a uniform fatigue top.

My only incident occurred during an exercise drill on the parade field. This particular exercise involved standing up straight with feet a comfortable distance apart and arms extended out, parallel to the ground. The hands then formed fists and turned in small circles first forward, then backwards. After several minutes of holding this position, the weight of one's arms becomes quite a strain on the shoulders. A drill sergeant walking in my direction approached me from the front and asked where I was from. He then said he hated everyone he had ever met from Illinois and punched me in the stomach, causing me to bend over and momentarily stop breathing. Thinking that my time for being singled out had come and gone, I was rather pleased and actually felt lucky that my turn was rather mild. But my time had not yet arrived.

It was quite cold that January morning, and it had been snowing intermittently for several days. As usual, it was chilly in the pre-dawn barracks. At 4:00 a.m., the drill sergeant announced morning by flipping on the lights and throwing a metal garbage can down the center aisle, its nasty contents leaving a trail as it rolled along. Moans and groans filled the room as feet quickly hit the floor. One man on a top bunk who hesitated on his mattress for a stretch was thrown onto the floor, bedding and all.

People raced around, heading for the showers, shaving, and getting dressed. By 4:30 a.m., all were dressed and ready for the day, with beds made up army style. My bunk was on top at the end of the row nearest the bathroom. The long window at the foot of the bed had a broken pane of glass, so on snowy, windy nights, the lower part of my wool blanket was covered by a skiff of snow, which usually dried out by evening.

After breakfast, several work details were assigned around the company area during the time before company formation. It was still snowing. Some troops were assigned to shovel the walks and others were cleaning up the garbage on the barrack floor. I felt lucky that I was assigned to buff the day room floor using an electric floor buffer. It was still dark outside when I finished and returned to the barrack. Most of the company was already starting to assemble in formation.

Not wanting to be last and risk being targeted by a drill sergeant, I quickly gathered up the items required for the morning activity, which was training on the proper erection of the military two-man tent. Each man had been issued a shelter half, which was a section of canvas that, when buttoned at the top with a buddy's shelter half, became a tent. One person kept the tent poles and the other kept the tent stakes. The shelter half was folded up neatly and stored as one of several items in the bottom of each person's metal wall locker. It was the same olive drab color as everything else.

Since I had an extra duffel bag and field jacket, it had been my goal to discreetly store them in the bottom of my locker by folding them slightly smaller than other items, including my duplicate duffel bag. Properly hidden in this manner, the extra duffel bag and field jacket had managed to go undiscovered during numerous inspections.

Reaching down to the bottom of my wall locker, I pulled out one duffel bag and stuffed into it the folding tent poles and what I thought was my shelter half. Then I grabbed my backpack and hurriedly left the darkened room for the company street, arriving just in time.

As the dark, gray sky slowly began to become slightly less gloomy, the company was marched to a training area about a mile away, arriving at a large, empty, snow-covered field. Orders were given, by platoon, to form rows of single lines from one side of the field to the other, with feet spread apart. Once these lines were formed, inspected, and found to be perfectly straight, the order was given to count off by twos. So, row after row, we counted off, our voices echoing sharply in the crisp morning air. This being done, the drill sergeant in charge ordered that each of the "ones" remove their bayonet from their pack belt scabbard and stick the bayonet into the snow immediately behind the left heel. The bayonet would mark the location of the front tent pole for each tent. The command was then given for each pair of men to erect their tent.

My bunk mate, the fellow who occupied the bed below mine, was a serious-minded person named John Wichmann from Portland, Oregon. He had been drafted into the army after dropping out of college.

We each picked up our duffel bag and shook the contents out onto the snow. From his came his shelter half and tent stakes. As I emptied mine, I was aghast to see my extra duffel bag fall out along with the tent poles.

"What's that?" John asked in wide-eyed horror, pointing towards the two duffel bags as if I had not yet perceived what he was getting at.

We both stared in disbelief at the pile lumped up on the snow while gradually coming to grips with what this moment meant in our lives, mentally playing out the dozens of possible outcomes, none of which were pleasant. John knew that I was a member of the Army National Guard and had not arrived at Ft. Lewis as a draftee. What he did not know was that these many weeks, I'd had an extra duffel bag stashed in my locker.

"Well, buddy," I explained, "my National Guard unit back home sent a duffel bag and field jacket along with me when I came here. I didn't really know what to do with them, so I had the extra duffel bag hidden in the stack of stuff in my locker. I was assigned to buff the day room floor this morning, and when I got back to the barrack, the lights were already off. In my haste to make the formation, I accidently grabbed my extra duffel bag instead of my shelter half."

John paused for a moment, first looking at me and then at the pile on the snow. "Well, why did you bring it out here?" he asked.

I had thought my explanation was clear and adequate, but perhaps John, whose mind might have been racing, had not captured all of my words. So I repeated a brief account of the facts.

"What are we going to do now?" he asked in a high-pitched, nervous tone.

It would have been fair for him to ask what I was going to do since it was my mistake causing the looming problem, but he had included himself in the question. I glanced back towards the rows of barracks, which could be seen on the bleak horizon, and said, "Maybe I can sneak off, go back, and get it." But then I realized that it would be much worse to get caught leaving.

So John and I just stood there. Maybe someone had brought an extra shelter half. Maybe I could fall over sick and be rushed away to sick call. Maybe a comet would strike Earth. Maybe no one would notice. Sure, and maybe this would be so bad that I would write a story about it many decades later.

That last possibility actually never crossed my mind. It might have if I hadn't been considering the likelihood of my impending attack by the drill sergeant.

Meanwhile, everyone else busily began putting up their tents, probably close to a hundred of them. John and

I were among the rows toward the back of the field, and I noticed the drill sergeants lingering together near the front. Perhaps thirty minutes went by. Neat, evenly spaced rows of olive drab tents began to arise out of the snow, all perfectly spaced, stark in appearance against the white background.

Having nothing else to do but worry, I soon realized that others were beginning to notice the obvious white, gaping space in one row with two motionless figures standing next to it.

The dreaded inevitable moment was about to come. I watched a drill sergeant stroll among the tents, inspecting the progress. "What's the problem here, men?" he asked when he reached us.

John quickly looked at me, knowing I would do the honorable thing and respond. So I began by explaining that I was an NG (National Guard member) and had been issued a duffel bag prior to entering basic training, which I kept in my wall locker. I spoke of my detail in the day room, the darkness in the barrack, and my haste to make the formation, all important and logical factors leading to the current situation. I spoke with care and confidence, man-to-man, which I hoped would be heard and understood by a reasonable man who could easily see that it wasn't entirely my fault.

I started to sense that my explanation had failed when he calmly asked me, "What is going on here?" as if my words had fallen into the deep snow between us, never reaching his ears.

I immediately began with the highlights: NG, extra duffel bag, day room, dimly lit wall locker. This seemed to irritate him. He rudely interrupted. "What's your name, troop?"

Still hoping to gain his mercy, I replied quickly with great respect for his presence.

The sergeant proceeded to unleash a significant castigation in my direction, closing the space between us with each word until he was so close to my face that each pore in his face, each blue dot denoting a shaved whisker, was observed by me. At the conclusion of this outrage, he commented on my questionable fitness for any human task. "Son, I want every man in this company to know what a dud you are. Pick up that duffel bag and hold it high above your head. Now I want you to yell as loud as you can, so that the entire company can hear you, and explain what you did."

I realized that my worst fears were now at hand. "I brought my duffel bag instead of my shelter half!" I yelled.

Explaining that not nearly all the company had heard me, he ordered me to repeat those words several more times. Finally, he acknowledged that I was just too far away for all to hear, so he suggested that I, with said bag held high, walk up and down each row of tents and tell every man, up close, what I had done.

The next hour was a daze as I complied. Thankfully, some troops did not pay any attention to me except for a quick glance. Others looked at me with a puzzled face and asked a question or two. Amidst this painful embarrassment,

I was at least glad to put some distance between myself and the hardened, uncaring sergeant who was surely among the hearing disabled.

At long last, I saw the mess hall truck in the distance heading to the training site. It was time for the morning soup break, as it was inaccurately described. It was the practice on cold days in the field for the army to provide a short break with a hot beverage. What was referred to as soup was actually a concoction of unknown origin consisting of hot salt water with miniscule particles or flecks of some substance that would swirl about when the "soup" was poured by a cook into your canteen cup, which was always carried on your backpack belt strap. The stratified particles in the liquid lacked density, and it was a rare occasion that said particles would sink to the bottom. But it was hot and at least provided some warmth to the cold, stinging fingers wrapped around the aluminum cup, itself a relic of WWII.

An announcement was made for the company to proceed to the mess hall truck and, with cup in hand, form a long line. I dashed back to my empty white spot, discarded the duffel bag, and followed the others. I breathed a sigh of relief as I sipped my hot salt water that had never tasted so good or provided such comfort. Upon slithering away from the truck, I intentionally employed my expert skills in becoming just another olive drab blob in a snowy mid-winter field somewhere in the seventy thousand acres that comprised Ft. Lewis. I picked out a large group of fellows huddled together in a tight group, holding their salt water and smoking cigarettes, which at that time were issued by the army with C-Rations. I didn't particularly recognize any of the fellows, but I thronged them tightly just the same.

Just as I began to relax, I heard a raised voice. "Where is that man who brought his duffel bag out here?"

Now it was my turn to feign deafness as I lowered my head and snuggled in among the other olive drab blobs as close as I could get. After hearing a drill sergeant continuing to ask about my whereabouts, I broke free of my cover and reluctantly walked over to the group of drill sergeants and officers standing together.

The one who had originally confronted me pointed out that the captain and first lieutenant were standing nearby. "I want you to go tell the company commander and first officer just what a dud you turned out to be."

Starting to get accustomed to the notoriety, I walked to where they were standing, engaged in conversation. Not wanting to interrupt, I stood there motionless until they began to notice me, first by quick glances as they spoke, then with longer looks. The captain finally stopped in the middle of a sentence, looked at me, and became silent. I reported that I had been instructed by a drill sergeant to inform him that I had brought my extra duffel bag to the field, rather than my shelter half.

Apparently, the commander suffered from the same hearing disability as the sergeant. "You did what?" he asked with incredulity.

I repeated my statement, which by now was on automatic pilot every time my mouth was open. He then inquired how such an event could transpire. "Sir," I said, "I am an NG and was issued a duffel bag by my home guard unit to be taken along with me to training. I had the bag stored in my wall locker and accidently grabbed my extra duffel bag rather than my shelter half in the dim light of the barrack." I further explained my haste and the day room buffing connection.

At that moment, I detected a small upward movement in one corner of his mouth. It could have been an expression of humor rather than disgust, or perhaps it had at long last occurred to him what the tiny particles were in the hot salt water beverage. Taking his softened expression as an indication that I might not be court marshaled before the day was out, I began to relax.

"You mean you were going to sleep in that thing?" he asked.

"No, sir," I said, remembering that this man had total twenty-four-hour control of my miserable life for some time yet.

"You know," the captain said, "I wonder if a man could sleep in a duffel bag. Go get yours and let's find out."

By the time I returned, the company had been assembled in formation, and it was announced that a soldier would demonstrate whether or not a duffel bag could be used as a shelter. Hundreds of eyes were on me as I was instructed to step inside the bag and pull it up.

After noting that the bag would only reach just past my waist, a voice behind me said, "Hmm, that doesn't work too well. Let's put it over your head and try it that way."

As instructed, I stepped out of the bag and lowered it down over my head. I found this moment to be somewhat comforting because the darkened interior of the bag muted the outside sounds, curbed the cold wind, and provided the illusion of solitude.

Finally, it was over. The formation was dismissed, and I was told to join my platoon, which I did with great dispatch. Later that night, and for a time thereafter, I was asked if I was that guy with the duffel bag. To many, I henceforth became known as the duffel bag kid.

I went on to finish basic training and then advanced infantry training, still cold, still hungry and miserable, but without much fanfare as others took their turn learning about the link between effective military training and humiliation.

I gained a new appreciation of many things that winter. Among them, I learned how you can still keep going on very little sleep and how you can be hungry all the time and still gain fifteen pounds, all the while reducing your waist size. But most of all, I learned the importance of blending in when among the other olive drab blobs.

CHAPTER

4

The Life of a Dog

 I SUPPOSE I SHOULD HAVE named her Dreamcicle, because that's pretty close to the color she was. Dreamcicles were a popular treat in my childhood. They consisted of an ice cream bar on a stick that could be purchased individually at most neighborhood grocery stores in the 1950s and 1960s. Their color was reddish-orange with a little white mixed in. If you were around in those days, you no doubt had one. Maybe you can still buy them today.

I named her Blu instead.

Her mother was a typical looking black lab with a little white on her chest. Her father was a Chow Chow, a rather stout, brownish-red fellow with long hair, known as a confident ladies man who roamed the mobile home court where my daughter Stephanie lived. Stephanie's

47

black lab was evidently smitten by Don Juan Chow Chow, and the result was a cardboard box full of puppies in her laundry room.

I always regretted not having my own dog as a boy. Timmy had his Lassie on TV, Roy Rogers and Dale Evans had Bullet, and Old Yeller was on the movie screen at the Saturday matinee down at the Arcadia Theater.

Dad had three beagles he kept in a fenced area near the garage and chicken house, but Buck, Shorty, and Lady were trained rabbit hunters and pretty much earned their keep when rabbit season started in November. With six kids in the family and only one wage earner, I could understand Dad's position that a dog just to follow me around was an unnecessary added expense. I asked permission to get a dog more than once, but to no avail.

By the time I arrived in high school, having a dog had become less important than having a part-time job and getting a driver's license. The busy years of college, starting my first job, getting married, and starting a family all resulted in the desire for a dog becoming only a faint memory. It was hard to find time enough to sleep as it was.

So I didn't get my first dog until I was forty-seven. By then my daughter Stephanie was out of school, living in her own home, and expecting her first son. She had acquired her female black lab about a year earlier and brought her over occasionally for a visit. After it was learned that the dog was with puppy, she and my wife, Amber, devised a strategy to entice me into getting my first dog at last.

Having become accustomed to peace and quiet returning to the house, I was not at first inclined to be receptive. The pups were born on August 25, 1995, and the first grandson, Tyler, came along five days later. Frequent visits to see the baby also involved visiting the six pups and their mother.

After rethinking the matter, I agreed to adopt Blu, and we brought her home when she was five weeks old. Of the six pups to choose from, three were black like their mother and three were the Dreamcicle color. Of those three, one seemed to stand out by being more alert, calm, and interested in human contact.

There's an old Appalachian song called "Old Blue" that I always liked. It is believed to have originated in the late nineteenth century, has many versions, and was first recorded in 1928. It has been done by many singers over the years, including Pete Seeger, Willie Nelson, and the folk group Peter, Paul and Mary. Its lyrics are simple and repetitive, but the melody is catchy and must have been written by someone who loved and understood dogs. One version begins with this:

I had a dog, his name was Blue,
I had a dog, his name was Blue,
I had a dog, his name was Blue,
Betcha five dollars he was a good dog too!

Even though Blu was a female and not blue at all, the name seemed to fit her. She did have bright blue eyes when she was born, but they turned brown by the time she was a few weeks old.

Wanting to be good dog owners, we soon purchased three books about dog care. One concerned what to do and not do to make a puppy a civilized part of the family. One covered how dogs think. And one was a book on teaching dogs tricks. I decided that I was not going to be Blu's master, but her roommate and friend, and I hoped that man and animal could develop a mutual respect. I learned later that, being an intelligent example of her kind, Blu had decided to keep her cards close to her vest for a while and size me up before making a commitment to becoming a civilized creature.

Things got off to a wonderful start. My wife, Amber, and I brought Blu home on Columbus Day weekend so we would have three days at home before returning to work on Monday. We had decided to dedicate all our time for those days to getting to know Blu and letting her get to know us.

Of course, advising her of the proper location for canine bodily functions was a focal point. We decided to offer a crash course and take her outside every two hours, night and day. At bedtime, we set the alarm clock to ring at two hours and took turns picking her up, carrying her outside, and setting her down in the grass. By Monday evening, she completely understood and was housebroken. Because she was my first dog, I didn't realize until years later that three days is a short time frame for this kind of success.

As the weeks rolled by, Blu quickly established herself as an important and lovable member of the household. I was amazed by how quickly she learned tricks. After only two or three tries, the basic moves of sit, shake, and stay were mastered. Once she learned something, she didn't forget it. She learned to drop down to the floor on command and roll over, and then she learned the low crawl. At the command to crawl, she would lie on her belly and pull herself across the floor. We practiced a couple of times a day, and she seemed to enjoy it as much as we did.

I called the local PetSmart store to schedule her for obedience training when she was four months old. The instructor said that a dog should usually be at least six months old before taking the training because younger dogs don't have the focus required to listen and learn. But he was willing to try it, so he signed us up.

Every Tuesday night we met at the store. The class was conducted toward the rear of the store near the big stacks of forty-pound bags of dog food. I was a little concerned that Blu might not socialize well with other dogs, especially older ones, but she did well. After several weeks of classes, the night for the final exam arrived. Each person took turns leading their dog through the various commands. Of course, Blu sailed through the test and, in my opinion, was valedictorian of the class.

It became our custom to take Blu for a walk to the park a few blocks away. When the weather was nice the following spring, Blu was nine months old, and we could hang out in the park for longer periods. Because she had learned the boundaries, we became comfortable with unsnapping her leash and letting her run free. She liked the kids who were at the playground and started to watch intently as they climbed up the ladder to the tall slide, sat down, and slid back down.

Watching her watch the slide gave me an idea. I put up our stepladder in the backyard and placed a dog treat on the first or second step. Soon Blu was able to stand on her hind legs to retrieve a biscuit. Next, I placed one out of her reach so she had to climb up the first step to reach the treat. It wasn't long before she could climb the ladder and get a treat off the top. She was nervous at first about what to do when she was at the top, so I would lift her off the ladder and put her back down. Later, she learned to just jump down by herself.

I wanted to try out her new skill at the park, so we walked to the park one evening after dinner and found several children playing on the slide. I took Blu to the bottom and said, "Up the ladder, up the ladder." Without hesitation, she climbed to the very top, which was twice the height of the stepladder. Once there, without stopping to look around, she sat down and slid to the bottom, much to the glee of the kids.

This became one of her favorite activities, and watching her was one of our favorites too. She would climb up and slide down several times along with the kids. She was getting to be a large dog by then, and it was comical to watch as she sat down at the top and whizzed down. The more we laughed and clapped, the more fun she seemed to have.

As the months and years passed, Blu repeatedly impressed us with her intelligence and agility. I had never thought about dogs having a sense of humor, but it was clear that she understood humor. If she did something we didn't expect and we laughed at it, she gave us a quick glance and did it again. Then she glanced at us again to see if we were laughing.

Blu liked the paperboy but disliked the mail carrier. Our newspaper arrived early in the morning and usually landed on or near the porch. Our routine for the paper fetch task was to open the front door and ask Blu to get the paper. She then ran outside and began her search. She first looked around the porch, and if she didn't see it there, she began her survey of the lawn until she found it, even if it was suspended in the bushes. While I held the door open, she rushed by me, the paper secured in her strong jaws, and gave it to Amber, who would be waiting in her chair.

Blu probably thought the mail carrier was a burglar who watched the house until we went to work and then sneaked around the front porch and tried to break in. She would bark and growl in a fierce manner that would have threatened me had I been the mail carrier. She successfully drove him away every morning, knowing that he would try to break in again the next day, necessitating her to appear vicious and save the day one more time. Sometimes when we were driving along a neighborhood street, she would notice a uniformed mail carrier a block down the street. At such times, she froze, stared down the street, and produced a long, low growl that sounded like it was coming from a much larger dog.

Over the years, our relationship with Blu was not one between dog and master. She was playful and got along well with everyone, but she retained her sense of self and independence. I always had the feeling that she would fulfill her role as friend to the family as long as she had her own space. I respected her as a living thing, no better or worse than myself, each with our right to give and take.

She had grown into a beautiful dog in her prime. Her coat was bright and thick, and she had a strong athletic appearance. Her chest and shoulders were muscular, and her rib cage narrowed down to a sleek torso. Her tail was bushy and curled up behind and over her back, and the white tip flashed in contrast to her Dreamcicle-colored coat, as did her snow-white underside. Her paws were not especially large, but they looked stout and matched her sixty-seven-pound frame.

Blu wasn't aggressive but thought of herself as the family's stoic protector. She reminded me of Teddy Roosevelt's foreign policy motto to speak softly and carry a big stick. During any relaxed family time, she would lie down with her back towards one or more family members and face away from them. At night, she slept on the floor with her back toward the bed and her head facing the doorway, ready for any abnormal sound or activity. This trait no doubt came from her Chow side, since that breed was originally used by the Chinese as guard dogs.

In 2001, when Blu was almost six, I retired and we moved to the country. Blu had grown up as a city dog, and I wondered if she would adjust to the fields and woods. But I need not have worried. Even though she was used to a fenced backyard and would now have sixty acres to explore, she seemed to be just as happy as I was to be there. She spent many hours trying to dig the muskrats out of their dens along the pond, chasing critters around the woods, and watching the hawks as they circled above. There were times when she came in at dark with her front half covered in mud from digging in the wet soil. She liked to leap from the stream bank behind the house into the muddy water and splash around to the other side.

One day not long after we moved to the country, we took a walk around the pond. Nearing the woods, Blu heard a noise and ran into the woods, out of sight. I waited a few minutes for her to return and was amazed to see her come walking out of the woods side by side with a wild turkey. They both walked up to me as if Blu were going to introduce me to her new friend. I held very still, and when they got close, the turkey turned around and walked slowly back into the woods. It was a mystery to me why a turkey and a dog would behave in such a manner.

Still, she watched over things. One day while working in our large lawn, I misplaced my favorite pair of loppers. I looked for them for quite some time, but they had seemingly disappeared. A day or two later, I was walking through the lawn near a row of trees and noticed them lying on the ground. In my excitement, I let out a shout, not realizing that Blu was just over the hill. She came running, stopped abruptly several yards away from me, and stared intently at my eyes with the wrinkled brow she only used in serious situations. She thought I was in trouble and needed her help. After watching me for a few seconds, she turned and walked back down the hill.

Blu had begun to show her age one hot summer, and we decided to have her hair cut short to keep her more cool and comfortable. The result was a drastic change in her appearance. Except for her head and tail, her coat was barely long enough to brush. With her coloring, she looked a lot like a lion. When we brought her into the house, she wandered around and acted a little strange. Then she walked into the bedroom and noticed herself in the full-length mirror. She looked at herself for a long time, wandered away, and sulked around the house for several days before she cheered up again.

As more grandkids arrived and came to visit, we were careful to monitor Blu's behavior. Being an older dog, she didn't like all the attention from the little kids, which included pulling, hugging, grabbing, and tugging at her. She could tolerate it for a while but would then quietly disappear to a hidden spot in the far reaches of the house.

It is just as hard to watch a beloved dog grow old and tired as it is to watch any human start to decline. By now, Blu had been in our family more than fifteen years, providing constant companionship and loyalty. She was no longer asked to perform tricks because it hurt her old bones to do so. After she had been napping, it sometimes took her several attempts to get up on her feet. The sight of a squirrel in the yard or a deer crossing the field no longer excited her. She slept more and more. Her eyes became cloudy and she couldn't hear her name when called. Still, she followed us around the house, rested nearby, and faced the door, her mind ready to push through her sore joints if she perceived a threat to the family.

The phrase "a dog is a man's best friend" originated from an 1869 court case in Missouri, *Burden v. Hornsby*, which went to the state supreme court the next year. Charles Burden's dog, Old Drum, was killed, and Lon Hornsby was sued for damages. Burden's attorney, George Graham Vest, won the case, and the judge awarded fifty dollars in damages. The following is his address to the jury:

The best friend a man has in this world may turn against him and become his worst enemy. His son or daughter that he has reared with loving care may prove ungrateful. Those who are nearest and dearest to us, those whom we trust with our happiness and our good name, may become traitors to their faith. The money that a man has, he may lose. It flies away from him, perhaps when he needs it the most. A man's reputation may be sacrificed in a moment of ill-considered action. The people who are prone to fall on their knees to do us honor when success is with us may be the first to throw the stone of malice when failure settles its cloud upon our heads. The one absolutely unselfish friend that a man can have in this selfish world, the one that never deserts him and the one that never proves ungrateful or treacherous, is his dog.

Gentlemen of the jury, a man's dog stands by him in prosperity and in poverty, in health and in sickness. He will sleep on the cold ground, where the wintry winds blow and the snow drives fiercely, if only he may be near his master's side. He will kiss the hand that has no food to offer, he will lick the wounds and sores that come in encounters with the roughness of the world. He guards the sleep of his pauper master as if he were a prince. When all other friends desert, he remains.

When riches take wings and reputation falls to pieces, he is as constant in his love as the sun in its journey through the heavens. If fortune drives the master forth an outcast in the world, friendless and homeless, the faithful dog asks no higher privilege than that of accompanying him to guard against danger, to fight against his enemies, and when the last scene of all comes, and death takes the master in its embrace and his body is laid away in the cold ground, no matter if all other friends pursue their way, there by his graveside will the noble dog be found, his head between his paws, his eyes sad but open and alert in watchfulness, faithful and true even to death.

In May of 2011, Blu was three months away from her sixteenth birthday. We had hosted a Mother's Day cookout at our house, and a large group of relatives was present. As the afternoon began to get hot, I led Blu to a place where she could be cooler and relax away from the younger children. After everyone was gone late in the day, I opened the door so she could wander around or nap in one of her favorite shady spots.

When we were inside after dark, I went out to let her in, but she wasn't there. After searching the immediate area, we returned to the house and got flashlights. We finally located her lying in a wet area of tall grass along the cornfield. Most of her body, but not her head, was in a shallow pool of water. She wouldn't get up at first, but with a little coaxing and help, she managed to get to her feet. She tried to follow us to the house but seemed confused and started to wander. When I snapped the lead on her collar, she was able to walk by my side if she leaned against my leg. As we neared the house, I picked her up. I carried her to her spot on the bedroom floor, laid her on her side, and offered her some water, which she was able to drink if I held it close to her head.

She seemed to sleep well through the night, and we called the veterinarian early the next morning, dreading the outcome, knowing that she'd probably had a stroke. I gently laid her in the back of the SUV for the drive to the office, and at our request, the vet came outside to the back of the SUV to examine Blu.

Dr. Hurliman, who was nearing retirement, concluded that she'd had a stroke and carefully chose his words. He left the decision up to us, but gently, kindly, and somberly led us to the obvious course of action, saying that Blu might not survive another week.

He left and returned with the necessary tools while we stayed to offer our old friend comfort as best we could. Although dizzy, Blu was sitting up with Amber's arms around her. Dr. Hurliman shaved a small patch of fur from Blu's front leg and placed the needle in a small vein of the friend who had journeyed with me from my forties to my sixties.

At that point, Blu calmly raised her old head and stared directly in my eyes. It was only a few seconds, but it seemed like a long time as a dozen different thoughts and emotions raced through me. Her questioning face reminded me of when she was a puppy, waiting for some word or guidance. Then she slowly lowered her head and lay down for the last time.

I returned with Dr. Hurliman to his office to write a check. Having a lump in my throat the size of a brick, I was hoping that he didn't want to talk. He mentioned something about the strength of the bond between humans and dogs, but I did not try to reply.

We buried Blu on a shaded hillside overlooking the small stream behind our house. I made a wooden marker for the grave, and I think of her to this day when I pass by, still silently and faithfully watching over her home.

One version of the ending of the "Old Blue" folk song is as follows:

When Blue died, he died so hard,
When Blue died, he died so hard,
When Blue died, he died so hard,
He shook the ground in my backyard.

When I get to Heaven, first thing I'll do,
When I get to Heaven, first thing I'll do,
When I get to Heaven, first thing I'll do,
Pull out my horn and call Old Blue
"Come on Blue you good dog you!"

5

Turbo Speed

THERE ARE TIMES IN A MAN'S LIFE when desires for modesty, privacy, and even dignity must be sacrificed for his own wellbeing and the greater good. These times may come unexpectedly or, if one is lucky, with a foreshadowing that allows time for mental preparedness. Sometimes matters of a more personal nature must take a backseat to the pressing matter at hand.

As a boy growing up in a small town long before video games, I had to be imaginative when hanging around the neighborhood with my buddies wishing for something to do. When long days really got slow, coarse bodily functions like flatulence and the potential woes of urinating on an electric fence to keep the livestock in check were not uncommon topics to joke about. Sometimes these entertaining discussions included a boast that a certain fellow could stand flat-footed and muster up enough propulsion to urinate completely over the top of an automobile car hood—no small feat when one considers the size of a car hood on a 1958 Cadillac. Although I never personally witnessed such a feat, fifty years later, I can't help but recall the possibility with some envy.

Like many male humans, I grew up oblivious to the aging process. At a youthful stage of life, it is easy to feel certain that grandfathers and grandfatherly figures exist to provide opportunities for stories, car rides, fishing and hunting events, and nickels and dimes for pop and ice cream. Older men were seemingly hardy and healthy, and from a boy's viewpoint, they had no problems with aging at all. Not once do I recall thinking about myself being called Grandpa someday or slowing down because lots of birthdays had passed. Subconsciously, I might have felt that even if that did happen far in the future, all the disadvantages of living more than sixty years would have long since been corrected.

Somewhere past the age of fifty, a former immortal boy begins to slowly accept that things are changing in an increasingly significant manner. Now young boys use the word Grandpa while looking squarely at you, and they expect, or at least hope for, car rides to interesting places as well as explanations of things you have long taken for granted. It is at this point that you notice that your hair is turning gray, you no longer feel like taking two steps at a time when bounding upstairs, you no longer skip the bottom rung when climbing down a ladder, and you no longer see the need to get everything done in the same day.

Then something happens that you don't expect, something that brings into focus the fact that it is now your turn to experience certain indications that you, too, might be showing signs of aging, and perhaps the causes of aging might not have been entirely eliminated in your lifetime after all.

This moment for me occurred about ten years ago during a long walk on an old roadbed with two young grandsons one sunny day. Stories were told and rocks were thrown from an old bridge over the creek. The several cups of coffee I'd had with Grandma at breakfast were nearing the completion of their own journey and needed a place to go. I suggested that the boys take a quick break while I stepped into the woods a minute to respond to nature's call. The youngest, Bradley, said, "Hey, I'll go with you. I have to pee too!"

As we stood side by side experiencing this little male bonding moment, I noticed that young Bradley had completed his task and had returned to the old road while I felt the need to linger a while longer.

When I too returned to the road, I said, "Boy, Brad, you got done twice as fast as me."

"That's because I put my pee on turbo speed, Grandpa!" he replied.

Well, that was it. I flashed back to a forgotten time long ago when I possessed the gift of turbo speed.

Have you ever noticed that something isn't troublesome until you notice it for the first time? And then you realize the problem arrived so gradually that you hadn't before recognized it as a problem—like when you first re-alize your neck doesn't turn quite as far around when you are trying to look behind you while backing out of a park-ing space, or when the podiatrist tells you that his dad, who is about your age, is having the same foot problem. It's that kind of thing.

As time went by, I noticed that I needed to get up more often at night to use the bathroom, something I found quite annoying, especially on cold winter nights when a cozy bed is such a comfort. I also noticed that com-bining bathroom stops only with fuel stops on long drives was a thing of the past and that rest area road signs were now a welcome sight.

Maybe the long endurance car trips of my youth had caused the problem. On family vacations, Dad was able to drive forever without a potty break, so pleas from the kids in the backseat were taken rather lightly. I recall having to go so badly that when I finally got the opportunity, it was difficult to commence the process. Yes, maybe I could pin the blame on him, rest his soul.

Or maybe it was that time in college when the pee was startled back into me. As serious-minded business ma-jors, we wore wingtip shoes and puffed on cherry blend to-bacco in hoping-to-look-like-Wall-Street-associates pipes. It was our custom to meet for coffee before our first morn-ing class in Blair Hall. On one such morning, I was in my marketing class with Professor Williamson suffering through great bladder pressure. Finally, the class ended. The restroom was right next door, so I zipped out of class, went around the corner, and stood before the nearest white porcelain fixture.

Professor Williamson, himself a person who appreciated a good cup of coffee, had also entered the restroom, unbeknownst to me. Suddenly, his deep, booming voice was right behind me. "Hello, Mr. Totten. How are you?"

The sudden surprise and interruption, along with the thunderous sound of his deep voice, caught me in midstream, so to speak, and the scare not only caused my relief to cease, but created some sort of reverse siphon, which in turn became quite uncomfortable. Perhaps my later issues could be traced to that unnatural trauma to my system.

At any rate, a trip to the urologist office—the site of the dreaded digital exam—was now in order. I was no stranger to this exam, having it each year as a part of an annual physical after I turned forty. For several years, my urologist had been a professor at the medical school in the city where I lived. His interns and students often accompanied him during his patient exams. The nurse escorted me to an examination room, and I waited quietly while gazing at the charts of the male reproductive and urinary systems that adorned the walls.

Eventually, the doctor burst in with great fanfare and greetings, followed by an intern wearing a white lab coat. In a polite but expectant way, he would ask if I had any objections to the intern observing the exam. Not being one to present myself as an obstruction to the advancement of medical knowledge, I always consented. Having gotten used to this drill, I suppose it was a small step when, on some visits, two or three interns followed the urologist into the room or when the doctor invited the intern to extend his latex-covered digit saying, "Well, Mr. Totten, your prostate appears to be somewhat enlarged and maybe a little bumpy. Would you mind if Intern Smith also examines you so he will know how to detect an enlarged prostate gland?"

I had first recognized the need for medical progress in my thirties when I experienced a series of prostate infections. I went to see Dr. Bland, my family physician at the time. I knew very little about this piece of my anatomy and wasn't even sure if it was properly referred to as the *prostrate* gland, as some older folks called it, or the *prostate* gland. Dr. Bland cleared up the confusion. He was a thoughtful, intelligent man with a good reputation and someone in whom I had complete confidence. After examining me, he scribbled out a prescription and instructed me to take two tablets a day for thirty days and return to his office once I had completed the regimen.

I did as instructed and returned for a follow-up visit. Seeing no improvement, another script was written for a different medication. After a few more weeks, I returned again and reported that the desired results had not been obtained. Of course, each visit included the infamous digital examination. This time, he instructed me to try yet another medication and call him directly one week later.

Still seeing no improvement, I phoned his office as requested and was rather surprised that he was available at that moment to speak to me. When he came to the phone, I identified myself and reminded him of his request to call, saying I was still having the same symptoms. A long pause then ensued. As the moments passed, I began to wonder if he was still on the line, but recalling his thoughtfulness, I saw him in my mind's eye poring through a medical journal, slowly turning the pages, and perusing each line for an answer until the next course of action became clear. At long last, he spoke, calmly saying, "Ain't that a bitch?"

The prostatitis infections eventually ended and twenty happy bladder years went by. But as time progressed and my trips to the bathroom became more frequent, I began to dread using public restrooms during events like plays, movies, and sporting events, especially when they were well-attended and there was a line waiting to use the urinals. Men might visit while in such lines, but once it is your turn to approach the urinal and unzip your trousers, there is a code of silence I never quite understood. Several men might be simultaneously using a row of urinals shoulder to shoulder, but they do so in complete silence, as if total focus is required to complete the process. Then, while the same gentlemen are washing hands at a row of lavatories, it is socially appropriate to commence small talk, saying something like, "Hey, that Beatles tribute band is really somethin', isn't it?"

These times of high demand for use of a urinal are what a man with a mature prostate gland fears. In my case, it took two to three times as long to complete the deed as it had in my youth. Sometimes even getting started was a slow process, and even then, minimal progress was made, and what progress was made included a few pauses. The

fellows on either side of me would come and go, obviously
still in possession of their turbo speed mechanism.

At such times, I speculated what the fellow right behind me thought. *Isn't this guy ever going to get done? Why
the hell did he get in line anyway if he didn't have to go? Sheesh!*

At some point, my doctor mentioned that some men
improve by taking an herb. I gave that a try for a couple
of years, but without much success. Next, he suggested
something newly developed called microwave needle
therapy. The mere mention of such a thing in connection
with that particular area of the anatomy would sound a
little touchy to even the toughest of rugged, hairy-chested
men. But the need for rapid and complete movement of
one's fluid intake can be even more pressing than the al-
ternative, so I scheduled the outpatient procedure.

As you might imagine, I arrived for the appointment
with some anxiety. The nurse ushered me back to a room
I had not seen on previous office visits that was connected
to the medical school. I could not decide if she was just
being friendly or if there really was a devilish gleam in her
eye. She instructed me to disrobe from the waist down,
put on a hospital gown, climb onto a table, and put my
feet into the stirrups. I had seen similar equipment in
rooms where babies were delivered, but I had never envisioned myself in such a contraption.

After what seemed like a long time, the nurse returned with the doctor. She said that my appointment co-
incided with his afternoon class and asked if I would mind
if the class came in to observe.

Many things went through my mind: What was the size of the class and its gender composition? Was my hospital gown positioned in a proper and discreet way? Where would the students be in relation to my exposed body parts? Would the procedure produce weird facial contortions or expressions in me? Still, not wanting to impede the progress and learning associated with ever-advancing medical technology, I agreed.

At that point, the doctor left the room and immediately returned with a mixed group of young men and women who were trying to display somber faces. I didn't count their numbers, but I suspect it was between seven and ten, not counting the nurse and doctor, who introduced me formally to the group and explained what medical issues were grounds for the wicked measures they were about to observe. Of course, it might have been the stress of the moment, but it seemed to me that the women in the class appeared more interested than their male associates, who no doubt were thinking this would make a good story later on over a few beers.

Next, the doctor removed the cover from a large machine with a thick electrical cord that ran into a wall outlet. The cord reminded me of the pigtail connection used with electric clothes dryers. A somewhat smaller cord extended from the front of the machine and traveled in a series of coiled loops to a large object that looked like a cross between a paintball gun and one of those large water guns kids play with on a hot summer day. Protruding from this handheld object with a trigger was a long metal rod with a pointed end that brought to mind a welding rod like the one I saw used to repair my tractor's broken snow blade. It flashed through my mind that the term *needle therapy* was a great misnomer arrived at by the manufacturer to provide no hint to the patient of what might be in store.

The machine was activated and made a high-pitched humming sound as if hundreds of volts of electrical energy were at its command. Then the doctor lubricated the "needle" welding rod with a substance resembling petroleum jelly and raised the hospital gown up to my waist, providing a clear and close view to everyone in the room of the primary decoration and its accessories. With that, the doctor inserted the rod what seemed like a couple of feet and turned up another numbered dial. "It will be pretty uncomfortable but won't last long," he said, then added, "and it will come and go at intervals."

He was right. Each time the level of discomfort rose to a peak, making me think that physical retaliation might be in order, it momentarily subsided only to rise again to a peak. It occurred to me that if this machine was suggested as a wartime interrogation device, it would surely be banned by the Geneva Convention. After what seemed an interminable length of time, the procedure was finally over, both for me and the future staff of a large hospital somewhere, a staff that would now know just what to do for patients with issues similar to mine.

The years continued to roll by, and I found myself enjoying great health into my retirement years, living far from the city. But as the years increased, so again did the number of trips to the bathroom. My latest urologist had limited me to one cup of coffee a day, throwing a wrench into my retirement plan to lounge the mornings away with friends at the coffee shop as we solved the country's political, social, and financial problems. Having already taken advantage of what had been the most current options a few years earlier, I was happy to hear that there was a new procedure, green light laser surgery, that I could avail myself of. Being asleep during that event, I have no idea how many bright, young interns I educated.

Sadly, the elusive turbo speed remains but a dream and a distant memory. It doesn't bother me, but I admit to an occasional feeling of envy when I happen to see a horse void with such force that he could be used to quell a prison riot. I have accepted the fact that I will never stand flat-footed and even come close to projecting a forceful arc into the air that crests the hood of even the lowest slung and smallest hybrid vehicle.

Some pleasures seem to be reserved for the young.

6

The Demise of Troop 314

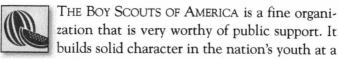THE BOY SCOUTS OF AMERICA is a fine organization that is very worthy of public support. It builds solid character in the nation's youth at a time when they are energetic and anxious to learn, have fun, and build relationships. It promotes self-reliance and independence. Gaining merit badges and achieving rank in the troop teaches a boy about working to achieve a goal while being guided by wise scout leaders, most of whom were once Boy Scouts themselves.

What local newspaper in small town America has not published articles about a grand deed being done by a solid young fellow who is working on his Eagle Scout project? It might be a new *Welcome to Farmsville* sign being erected on the main artery into town, or a pair of benches for the courthouse lawn where seniors can visit about the good old days, or a fundraising activity for a monument at the city park.

Even many former presidents gained some of their high ideals and leadership experience as members of some small town troop of the Boy Scouts of America. There is little doubt that reciting the Scout Oath and Scout Law has filled many a malleable son with a lofty sense of doing the right thing . . . and maybe even becoming a hero by dragging an old lady from a burning building.

Unfortunately, despite the efforts and best intentions of parents and Scoutmasters, things sometimes go awry. Although creating a cornucopia of memories, the zealousness and quest for fun by boys can cause a frustrating experience for dedicated Scoutmasters, not to mention a gross deviation from their plans, based on the tenets of the Scout Oath and Scout Law. Such was the case in the untimely demise of Troop 314.

The local American Legion Post, another fine organization, was the sponsor of Troop 314 in my hometown, and meetings were held once a week on Wednesday evenings. At that time, the Legion was a brick building with a finished lower level. Scout meetings were at 7:00 p.m. upstairs in a large, open room that encompassed the entire floor, which was used for Legion post gatherings such as weekly dances and special dinners or "feeds."

Meetings began with Scoutmaster Dan Regain, along with one or two assistant Scoutmasters and senior patrol leader Jerry Crites, gathering the Scouts in a circle. Announcements were made concerning future troop campouts, progress toward merit badges, uniform issues, and the schedule for the evening. There might also be an introduction and swearing in of new troop members.

Following this, the troop would separate into assigned patrols, each with a higher-ranking Scout holding the title of patrol leader who took and reported attendance and facilitated individual work on merit badges. Patrol leaders normally held the coveted rank of First Class or above. In this regard, I suspect that Troop 314 was similar to most other troops in the country in the late 1950s.

After the conclusion of the business portion of the meeting, a scout leader would make the exciting announcement to wrap up whatever was being done because it was time for midnight football. This game consisted of dividing the troop into two teams, which, depending on the evening's attendance, could result in as many as twenty team members on each side.

As in football, a line was drawn down the center of the room, with a set of objects at each end that represented goalposts. The two teams then assumed positions on their hands and knees, facing each other at the centerline. With the teams thusly positioned, all lights were turned off, resulting in such darkness that it was difficult to perceive which Scout was next to, in front of, or behind another Scout.

At this time, a scout leader would toss a "football," which was actually a small object of some sort, in the direction of the center of the dark-as-midnight room. The first Scout on either team to grab the "ball" would then move forward, attempting to carry the ball through the line of the opposing team members and then across the goal line, thereby scoring a touchdown. After a touchdown was scored, the ball would again be tossed into the air and the process begun anew.

During this game, an impartial observer might discern an abnormality in typical Scout troop behavior. (A Scout is kind.) Whether it be throw-caution-to-the-wind aggressive behavior, an overflow of competitive spirit, or the mixing of a delicate balance of personalities, midnight football was rough. As a player hiding the football under his shirt attempted to make his way toward the goal line, he might be preyed upon in a most convincing manner by another player in an effort to gain control of the ball. A younger Tenderfoot Scout waiting for his next growth spurt might suddenly feel the crushing pressure of a much larger and older First Class Scout bearing down upon his person. Even a mild-mannered Scout skirting the fringes of the floor might be mistaken for a ball carrier and pounced on. With visibility poor, a fellow team member could easily be mistaken for an opponent player and accidently converged upon.

I have since wondered what such a commotion must have sounded like to the World War II veterans in the bar one floor below who were trying to enjoy a Falls City or Carling's Black Label beer while scores of knees and hands were beating the floor above their heads. (A Scout is courteous.) Perhaps some were reminded of mortar rounds exploding on a European battlefield. Others might have wondered why they had voted in favor of the post sponsoring a Boy Scout Troop in the first place.

It was a rare meeting when a close inspection of Troop 314 during the last formation did not reveal a few torn uniforms, missing buttons, or red rashes from headlocks. But all was forgiven, and each Scout headed out into the night air convinced that he was lucky to be part of the best troop in town.

Other than weekly meetings, the primary activity of Troop 314 was camping. Several overnight campouts were held each summer at various locations. Although the troop was located in a southeastern Illinois town, it was part of the Buffalo Trace Council, which was headquartered in neighboring southern Indiana, so many campouts were held in that state.

One particular trip scheduled in the fall of 1959 required travel to Camp Arthur, located about forty miles away, north of Vincennes, Indiana. The event began quietly enough with Scouts meeting at the American Legion at 9:00 a.m. on a Saturday morning. The usual camping gear and food were loaded into vehicles, and the adventure began. What would seem like a quick trip now—twenty-nine miles to the state line—felt much longer then.

That part of Indiana was then, as it is now, known for the production of fruits and vegetables by small farms and individual homeowners who had a few acres in the country. The sandy soil was particularly conducive to growing watermelon, cantaloupes, and pumpkins. A Sunday drive in the fall to visit the many roadside produce stands is still popular today. One could not do better than cut into the luscious red innards of a prized Indiana melon.

A large watermelon field did not go unnoticed as Troop 314 reached a point within a mile of Camp Arthur.

The gravel road wound through a hilly and mostly wooded area, culminating at the camp's seven acres, which contained dirt roads and trails with clearings among the trees that were designated for tent camping.

The vehicles were quickly unloaded, the troop was divided up by patrol units, and camp was pitched. Army surplus pup tents, each housing two Scouts, were put up in a semicircle. We gathered wood so each patrol could start a campfire and cook lunch. Each Scout was instructed to bring enough food from home for one person. We complied. (A Scout is obedient.) On campouts, the standard fare was a package of hot dogs and a package of buns, a can of pork 'n beans, and maybe some apples or a candy bar.

Fires were something of a troop specialty. The Scout handbook described in detail the various kinds of campfires and their uses, including windbreaks and heat deflectors. You could build a small bonfire by arranging the kindling twigs and larger pieces in a teepee shape to create a tall, bright fire or dig a hole and start a pit fire, which you could cook on using a bed of red, glowing coals. Of course, the campfire became the gathering place and focus of socialization after dark. (A Scout is friendly.)

During the afternoon, discussion turned to the watermelon patch. Most of the Scouts had never seen one, and it was rather a novelty to see so many watermelons in one place, randomly scattered in a field. It was probably one of the Harmon brothers, Freddy and Jerry, who first suggested that a big watermelon would be mighty tasty around the campfire after dark.

The Harmon boys were well known throughout the troop as energetic innovators, full of confidence and creativity that was not always channeled to good use. Jerry, the older of the two, was a risk taker before the term was in popular use, and he was not known to think things through, preferring to spring into action before too much thought could make him pause.

Freddy was of smaller stature and thrived on coming up with witty and humorous ideas. Many campout actions that strayed from the strict adherence to the Scout Law could be traced back to Freddy or Jerry.

At first, the proposal for procuring the succulent fruit involved only one or two Scouts who would wait until dusk to avoid being missed by anyone. Then they would follow the road back to the patch and secure one melon, maybe two, which would result in an evening treat for the patrol. But word spread quickly around the camp that a clandestine raid was afoot, and soon members of other patrols were involved. While not everyone in the troop was privy to the plan, a large delegation did become interested.

Once camp was set up, it was common for the Scoutmaster and other leaders to keep to themselves in an area set apart from the patrols. In fact, we rarely interacted with leaders at all between dusk and dawn. It could be that this was intentional to encourage the development of self-reliance. The members of Troop 314 wanted to do the right thing. (A Scout is trustworthy.) The quest for adventure and fun did, however, make some Scouts be easily misled by more persuasive personalities.

It was luck that a full moon began to rise that night, or perhaps that fact played a part in the motivation for the havoc that later ensued. The fall sun had barely dropped below the horizon when the Scouts on the secret watermelon detail began to assemble. Several had suggestions on a group strategy for a successful reconnaissance mission, but no clear group leader emerged.

At any rate, the contingency quietly strolled off together in a manner that would suggest an effort to gather some firewood for the night or enact a "snipe hunt" on some poor Tenderfoot Scout.

The dusty, winding road back to the watermelon patch seemed like only a short hike at first. Upon arrival, the patch appeared much larger than first thought and was bulging with large, light-green striped melons. The moonlight lit up the field, and the sight of it was the stuff from which legends are made, thus creating a memory to be shared for years to come with neighborhood buddies. (A Scout is loyal.) The once bushy green vines had mostly dried and turned yellow, leaving those heavy green torpedoes of pleasure basking in the cool glory of a perfect autumn evening.

The selection process was begun at once. Many employed the accepted and time-proven thump test, which involved a pronounced strike of the melon's center with the end of the largest digit of the hand. If the sound was less than the desired deep, hollow sound, the prospect was forgotten and the search continued until the exact preferred sound was obtained.

Once the selections were complete, the group informally gathered back on the road for the march home. Some participants, especially those of smaller stature, had just one melon in hand, while stronger and more determined fellows hoisted two.

The hike back began with the good humor of those who are imagining the pleasures that would follow, thanks to their efforts. (A Scout is cheerful.) But it soon became clear that carrying two large, heavy watermelons was not an easy task. Each was approximately eighteen inches long and weighed perhaps twenty-five pounds, but some might have been quite a bit heavier. It wasn't long before grunts and moans became audible, occasionally followed by the sound of a treasured piece of produce hitting the earth.

Camp Arthur, with its pleasantly inviting campfires, started to seem like miles away. As we crossed a bridge over a muddy creek, one of my melons slipped off my shoulder, bounced off a wooden bridge plank, and landed with a splat in the deep mud at the water's edge, almost burying it entirely. It crossed my mind that I could scamper down the bank under the bridge and recover it. (A Scout is thrifty.) But carrying the remaining one seemed a lot more comfortable.

Even though the canopy of trees shaded the moonlight here and there, the carnage of broken watermelons left on the trail became quite noticeable.

By the time we reached camp, no one was carrying more than one melon. In fact, some of the smaller boys were no longer carrying any at all. It was now well after dark, and the boys who had remained were gathered around their campfires. The excursion's bounty was distributed and consumed, and the first stories of the great raid were told.

Maybe having a taste of a life of crime encouraged other questionable acts as the evening wore on. Someone mentioned how funny it would be to sneak unseen, under cover of darkness, into another patrol area and place remaining pieces of watermelon in sleeping bags while the bags' unsuspecting owners sat visiting around a fire. This might have been a chance to get even for some act of midnight football aggression. Wouldn't it be a surprise—and so funny—if someone crawled barelegged into a sleeping bag only to find cold, wet chunks of watermelon? Imagine their reaction! Targets were identified and the deeds were done.

A Scout familiar with the physics of heat expansion came up with another trick. "Hey, did ya' know that if you bury an unopened can of pork and beans in the coals of a campfire, it will heat up and explode?" he asked.

"Yes, that's right!" another said in agreement.

"Let's wait until people are gone from their campfire and then sneak in and bury some cans in the coals," the first suggested.

Again, this idea gained acceptance and actions were taken.

Later that night, after most Scouts had gone to bed—some making the best of it after casting out as much melon as possible from their still damp bag—another prank was devised to be played on John McKnight. John was known as the soundest sleeper in the troop. He retired early and once asleep, he could not be easily awakened. He was always the last to get up in the morning, not caring if breakfast was ready or if the troop was breaking camp. No one cared to share a tent with John because of his fondness for slumber, so he was accustomed to having a tent to himself.

"Let's quietly pull up John's tent stakes and drag him in his tent out into the woods," someone, probably a Harmon, suggested.

I don't mean to pick on the Harmons here, but it was a classic Freddy idea.

A small group of volunteers located the tent, pulled the stakes, grabbed each corner of the tent, and carried the sleeping fellow out into the woods. Of course, when the tent was moved, the supporting end poles collapsed and the canvas roof then rested on the occupant, a change that had no effect on him whatsoever. He remained asleep.

Many dastardly deeds are eventually discovered in the light of day, and ours were no exception.

The bright morning sun soon began to illuminate the wanton results of Scouts run amuck. A mess of broken watermelons and rinds littered the camp randomly. The roofs of some tents had noticeable burn holes in them resulting from hot coals being launched into the heavens and raining down upon them. Even the attire of some Scouts showed blackened holes and the remnants of flying scorched beans, which would later require explanations to parents. (A Scout is brave.)

Soon rumors originating from the Scoutmaster's quarters spread around the troop. Evidently, the owner of the watermelon field had discovered the raid as well as the trail of broken watermelons leading directly to camp and was demanding to be made whole.

As the troop began to pack for the trip home, someone remembered John McKnight, who had not yet been seen. A search was made. (A Scout is helpful.) The sleepy-eyed, confused looking John was found, far into the woods, just emerging from his crumpled tent.

The winter of 1959-1960 passed without a notable event. Weekly meetings at the American Legion resulted in several merit badges being awarded. I had progressed from the rank of First Class to the rank of Star. Former Webelos Cub Scouts were now old enough to become Tenderfoots and join the troop. Midnight football continued to cause rough behavior and maybe some bruised and sore bodies. Although the biggest perpetrators could not be identified, rumors of persons of interest abounded.

The biggest event in the Scout year was the weeklong stay at Camp Pahoka in southern Indiana. It was an event we all looked forward to. Merit badge classes were held there, and an industrious scout could begin and complete all the work necessary to add a few new patches to his uniform. Additionally, many activities were available, including archery, rifle range shooting, fishing, swimming, canoeing, and compass navigation.

The camp itself was large enough to accommodate many different troops from different areas of southern Illinois and Indiana. Each troop site was provided cots for sleeping and large four-man tents supported by wooden frames. The tents were arranged in two rows divided by an open area. Some had an open shelter area for troop activities and a flagpole. A large mess hall with a kitchen was located a block away. A canteen where snacks could be purchased was on the main street, and there was a chapel for Sunday services. (A Scout is reverent).

The week leading up to the ultimate demise of Troop 314 began at Camp Pahoka in August of 1960. As usual, parents volunteered to transport the Scouts to and from the camp, and the activities began normally enough. It wasn't long, however, before the monster of miscreant behavior raised its head.

Although I admit that I was a participant in the Great Watermelon Raid of 1959, I do not admit being a contributor to the troop disintegration at Camp Pahoka. In fact, I would like to think that my days of being easily misled were over by then and that I had matured into a serious, model Scout, although I have not yet saved anyone from a burning building.

Not being involved in the misdeeds at Pahoka, I can only speculate about the final straw, but I know that late-night gambling and cigarette smoking were involved. At dusk, Scouts from all troops marched to the main flagpole near the canteen. We stood motionless and quiet as the colors were lowered and the flag was folded. Someone with a bugle performed taps. Bedtime was 10:00 p.m., but a group of rebels stayed up very late in one or two tents to play poker, gamble for money, and smoke cigarettes. I highly suspect the Harmon brothers were involved.

These dens of ignominy were located fairly close to the scout leaders' tents. One night, I opened the flap to one of these tents and thick smoke hung in the air, causing any respectable Scout to gasp for breath. There was also a mumbling of what was probably foul language too.

It was during that camp that it became popular to de-pant unsuspecting Scouts. A group of roving fellows would spy a lone Scout innocently traveling through the camp. The group would overpower the Scout, remove his trousers, and then raise the garment to the top of the flagpole. De-panting was particularly troublesome because the victim had to retrieve his drawers while surrounded by jeers from others.

Just past the middle of the week, I noticed that something was afoot throughout the camp. Small groups of Scouts had formed here and there, and serious facial expressions were noted. Joining a group, I was shocked to learn that the Scoutmaster, overwhelmed with bad behavior in the troop, both from the previous fall campout and this one, had quit and already gone home, leaving assistant scout leaders in charge. Parent drivers had been summoned to come to Indiana and transport the Scouts home. Even though the week was not yet finished, Scouts were told to pack up and prepare to go home. Troop 314 had come to an end.

There was another Scout troop in town, and a few Scouts might have migrated there, but as far as I know, the scouting career was over for most members of Troop 314. Items of uniform (including ones with burn holes) were later seen for sale at garage sales. Wednesday night rumblings of midnight football were heard no more on the second floor of the American Legion Post 30.

Fifty-five years later, it is interesting to think about what became of the troop members. I would like to think that many support scouting today. I know that some have gone to that great Scout jamboree in the sky. All those I am aware of grew up to be good, productive citizens. Most are now grandparents and have retired. I wonder if they ever think of the Scout Oath and Scout Law and recall living in a time when the world was a simpler, safer place and anything really fun involved being outside.

I also wonder if they, as I, have developed a lifelong fondness for the taste of green-striped watermelons.

CHAPTER

7

The Old Well

 AIDEN HAD ALWAYS HAD A KNACK for details and remembering things, even things that were not important to remember. Things just entered his mind, found a comfortable corner, and took up permanent residence, only to peek out through a window when they heard their name.

Sometimes it was a good thing, like when he remembered the parts number on a worn out oil well pump jack or the variety of tomatoes that he really had good luck with in his garden three years ago. Other times, small facts that would never be useful again would rest forever on the back porch of his brain, like the phone number of his grandparents, who had both been gone for many years. It was a gift when he was able to recall something pleasant or needed and a curse when something reminded him of a sad moment.

Even now, exhausted and drifting off in a calm, dream-like state, eyes closed, his mind was poking around its file cabinet, unwilling to sleep. Each thought, like autumn leaves falling from a tall tree, floated randomly, drifting here and there on a quiet breeze, separate but sometimes almost intersecting until each gently landed on the earth and became indistinguishable from the others, forming a soft blanket, whose job it was to cover a lifetime.

It had been a particularly long, hot, early summer day. Working in the oil fields of southeastern Illinois had always been a physically demanding job, and the weather was a big factor in how any day would end. During the unusually cold previous winter, the truck barely started on some mornings. The dirt roads leading to the wells would start out frozen solid and white with frost, but by mid-morning, they would thaw out just enough to create a thin layer of slick mud on top so that even the most aggressive tires would lose traction and slide off into the deeper ruts. Valves on the pump jack and pipelines were sometimes frozen and difficult to open and close. Spring weather presented new problems that often required leaving the truck on a gravel road and hauling out the ATV from the truck bed.

But right now it was the heat, and folks were using words like muggy, close, and sticky. If that were not enough, the mosquitos were as bad as they get. But after seventeen years as a pumper, Aiden was used to the highs and lows of the job.

The day had begun normally. Aiden had gotten up at 5:15, turned on the coffee pot, and gone out to the garden to check his tomato plants. He didn't really have a hobby, but he enjoyed growing a large patch of tomatoes, way too many for a single guy and his mother. It was not unusual for him to have more than fifty plants of a dozen different varieties. He particularly liked the ones that produced very large tomatoes, like Big Boy, Better Boy, and Beefsteak, although the old traditional Rutgers and Early Girl plants produced fine, deep-red, round tomatoes. Some plants were in cages, some were staked, and others were allowed to vine around on the ground.

Although uncomfortable to work in, the hot, humid weather and warm nights were making the plants thrive and grow quickly. He could see that he had planted most of them too close together, which was going to make them more difficult to pick. His mother canned some of them and made tomato juice, but mostly, he gave them away to neighbors and relatives.

He returned to the old farmhouse where he and his mother lived and found her up and in the kitchen frying bacon. He had told her he could fix his own breakfast, so she didn't need to get up, but she said she enjoyed getting up early. It occurred to him that he didn't tell her how much he appreciated her enough. His dad had died two years earlier, and he wondered if she really did like getting up early to fix him breakfast or if she was just being nice and secretly wished she could sleep late.

After eating, Aiden started the truck, turned south at the first corner, and drove by the old house site and farm that had been home to his grandparents. As the crow flies, the old farm was about half a mile from where he lived and could be seen from his tomato patch. His brother-in-law now farmed the acreage there, and Aiden helped to maintain the two old barns near where the old house had been. He was surprised to see that the grass was getting tall so quickly and decided to go over after work and mow it, a task he rather enjoyed. His brother-in-law had been wanting to clear off the site, except for maybe the best barn, and farm over it, but Aiden, being more nostalgic, wanted to preserve the site.

As a boy, he had spent many days there with his grandparents. It had been their home for over sixty years, and it almost seemed disrespectful to clear it off, as if to do so would detract from their memory. Besides, he felt close to them when he mowed and thought they might be smiling down on him.

As he drove to his first lease site, the sun was up and it was already hot. It crossed his mind to maybe turn on the air conditioner, but he decided it wasn't worth it. He would be in and out of the truck all day, and it seemed like the heat was worse when he stepped out of the cool truck cab into the sultry, oven-like air.

There was very little shade anywhere on his route. Most oil wells were drilled on farm ground with a lease road providing access, which meant driving along or through a corn or soybean field. Corn was the worst for heat because once it got tall, very little air moved through the stalks, and the humidity seemed to hang there in pockets around the pump jack.

The first three locations were operating normally and only needed a quick check, but the next two were silent, not pumping. He restarted the motor quickly on one, but the other took over an hour to get going again, a delay that put him behind schedule the rest of the day. In the afternoon, another three locations were in bottom ground still muddy from spring rains, so he had to use the ATV to get down to the pumps.

The back of his truck was a mess with oil covered tools, a toolbox, old rags, a few pieces of lumber, and the ATV, which barely fit. Although he knew he was getting lax about it, he knew it was safer to park the truck on fairly level ground before unloading the ATV. There are many hazards in oilfield work, but unloading the ATV was a minor one. Aiden would set the ends of the metal ramps on the back of the truck, climb up into the bed, and then sit on the ATV seat and back the vehicle backwards down the ramps. The first few times he did this, it had felt awkward to start down the ramps and quickly descend to the ground. Having repeated this procedure hundreds of times now, it felt very safe. The ramps had slipped off the truck a couple of times when he started out a little fast, but the ATV just fell to the ground, bounced a little, and presented only a small danger as long as he held the handlebars tightly. The worst part today was sitting on the hot vinyl seat until it cooled off, but the ride down the lease road to the well was enjoyable.

The steamy day wore on as the route progressed. Around 11:30, he took a few minutes to park in a shady spot and open his lunch bucket, which he had packed the night before and placed in the refrigerator along with a thermos containing a gallon of sweet ice tea. It was then that he noticed the wild tiger lilies were in full bloom. He had often wondered how the bright orange flowers had ended up growing along so many country roads. Perhaps they were popular among nineteenth century farm wives and had eventually spread to roadsides. Many old farmhouses had a row of them in the yard, even when the house had been long gone. A patch of them was still growing near some old silver maple trees near the spot where his grandparents' home had been.

Gene, Aiden's father, had also been a pumper, in addition to being a part-time grain and hog farmer. It had been an easy path to follow in his footsteps. Not only was Aiden the youngest in the family and the last sibling still living at home, he had ridden along with his dad some during the summers when he was growing up. He had learned enough that he could fill in for his dad when he first got sick. No one knew that he would be sick for such a long time and never recover.

This year, Aiden's route was 270 miles a day. He did not have a set starting and quitting time, and to some extent, he could set his own schedule. He was expected to check each well each workday, but he could change the order in which he checked them. The time at which he finished his route was almost never the same two days in a row because it depended on what was needed at each location. On a good day, most leases needed little or no attention, and he could arrive home by 3:00 p.m. On a rough day, when the roads were bad and several locations needed some work, his work-day could be two hours longer. On the infrequent occasions when he came across an oil leak at a pump, transfer pipe, or storage tank, his day might extend to almost sunset.

It was a good job for the most part, and it paid better than many jobs in the county. As long as he did his job, no one bothered him or looked over his shoulder. He checked with his boss when a special problem arose, but otherwise, he might not see him for weeks. Some would consider the work solitary and lonely, but he liked it.

Aiden arrived home about 3:45 and parked the truck in the drive beside the house. As he walked around to the back of the house, he saw that his mother was in the small garden pulling green onions to go with supper. Even though the front of the house faced the road, the front door was seldom used. The back porch was the place to leave muddy boots or oil soaked hats and clothes at the end of the day. Aiden pulled a paper towel from his pocket that he had carried since lunch and wiped the sweat from his forehead. "This has got to be one of the hottest days of the year," he said, mostly to himself but loud enough for his mother to hear.

"Go in the house and sit in front of the fan to cool off until supper is ready," she replied.

"No. I want to run over and mow at Grandma's place before I eat, and then I'll be back and won't have to go back out again," he said.

"Okay, son, but don't be too long. I want to be done cooking as early as I can so the house will cool down be-fore bedtime."

He agreed to make it quick and headed for the pole barn to get the tractor.

The Allis-Chalmers was old and looked old. The once bright red paint was now very faded and mixed with rust, resulting in a dull, brownish-orange color. It still ran fine most of the time, though, and was still useful as long as you didn't expect too much out of it. He recalled when his dad had bought it used at an auction some thirty years ago. The five-foot bush hog rotary mower was already attached to the three-point hitch, so Aiden lost no time in starting the engine and heading down the dusty gravel road.

After rounding the corner and heading south, he got a brief break from the hot late afternoon sun because it was shaded by a long row of old walnut trees. His grandfather had planted the trees as a young man, and Aiden wondered what he would say about them now if he could see their thick, strong trunks and large crowns. He could see the walnuts forming on the branches, and they looked to be no bigger than marbles.

After pulling into the old house site, Aiden put the tractor in neutral, engaged the power takeoff, shifted into gear, and slowly released the clutch until the blades of the mower began to spin. He set the mower height to about four or five inches and began to mow. He usually began mowing on the outside edges of the three-acre house site, mowing in towards the center, thereby keeping the number of tractor turns at a minimum. It was fairly easy mowing except for along the old barns and around the maple and walnut trees where it was sometimes necessary to drag fallen branches out of the way first. This time, he mowed directly across the center of the lot, where the old house had once stood.

As he returned from the first pass, he noticed some old fence posts lying in a pile with weeds almost waist-high around them. He decided to hop off the tractor and stack the posts against the barn so he could mow straight through rather than mow around the pile. He depressed the clutch pedal and disengaged the mower, shifted to neutral, hopped down off the tractor, and grabbed two posts. Feeling a splinter digging into the palm of his hand, he dropped the posts and returned to the rear of the tractor to get a pair of gloves from the small toolbox behind the seat.

As he headed back to the posts, he started to step over the old hand-dug water well that had been covered for many years. But as he moved, his ankle caught in some weedy vines, which in turn shortened his step. It happened so quickly that he didn't have time to comprehend the impact of what it meant as his foot landed soundly on the center of the well. The rotten wooden well cover made a slight cracking sound and collapsed, instantly dropping him down into the well.

At first, he didn't realize what had happened, as he gasped at the shock of the cold water surrounding his body. A second later, he felt a profound wave of embarrassment and fear flooding his mind. He instinctively reached up to grab the top of the well and was horrified to realize that he could not reach it. That realization, coupled with being encompassed by the cold water, which was an icy contrast to the hot, humid air a moment before, created an avalanche of panic during which he thrashed wildly about, kicking his legs and reaching his arms desperately above his head.

Then his focus returned. Realizing that he had to evaluate the situation, he drove the panic from his mind. At first it seemed very dark in the well, but he could now see the round outline of the well's top and the summer sky above that. He became aware of the sound of the tractor running nearby. Feeling embarrassed again, he thought about how silly it would be to crawl out of the hole, soaking wet and cold on such a hot day. Some neighbor driving by might have already noticed the tractor running and wondered why it had been left running with no one around. He hoped he could get out of the well before someone did come along so he could at least gather his wits first.

He stretched his legs downward as far as he could. By pointing his toes downward, he thought he could almost detect a solid bottom, but he could not quite get enough support to hold his body up. Looking up, he could see what appeared to be a board partially extending over the top of the well, silhouetted against a rounded view of the blue sky above. If he could just raise himself up high enough to grab that board, maybe he would find it still attached to a remaining section of the well cover, and he could use it to pull himself the hell out of there.

So he devised a plan to kick as hard as he could with his legs while simultaneously thrusting his arms upward.

With great effort, he kicked wildly and reached up with all the strength he could muster. His fingertips touched the board, but he could not close his hand around it. As his body fell downward, his head dropped below the cold water, causing the panic to return for a moment. Luckily, he was holding his breath during his lunge upward, so no water entered his mouth or nose. He noticed that his fingertips were clawing the sides of the well and that he had a glove on one hand and none on the other. Frantically thinking that he could get his fingers around that board easier if the glove was off, he pulled the glove off with his teeth instead of using his ungloved hand so he would not lose contact with the side of the well.

Calming slightly, he mentally prepared to exert the maximum amount of effort to reach the board. Again, his fingertips touched the board but could not hold on. The attempt resulted in him banging his elbow on the side of the well, temporarily rendering the arm useless, which again conjured up panic.

Not until this moment did Aiden realize that he might be in serious trouble. He had never learned to swim but could dog paddle if he needed to. The inside of the well was lined with rows of bricks, and he could see that some were uneven with varying amounts of mortar between each row. He also noticed that one brick protruded out a little farther than the rest. Quickly cupping his hands, he placed the fingertips of both hands just above this brick, and by pushing down, he was able to hold some of his weight, which allowed him to relax his body somewhat and rest.

He held this position for several minutes while he again considered what to do.

He could still hear the tractor running a few feet from the top of the well, although he thought that it did not sound quite as loud as before. He also noticed how cold the water was and recalled drinking at the well with his grandfather when he was a young boy. Back then, the well was covered by a slab of concrete that had a hole in the center where the hand pump rested. Hanging from a post near the pump was a metal cup tied on a cord to use for a drink of cool well water and a small container of water to use when the pump needed to be primed. He had never wondered about the well or asked his grandparents, who had originally dug it. He had never thought about how a well would be dug by hand or considered that it might be lined with bricks. Yet, here he was, clinging to the edge of a single mislaid brick that had not been touched since some unnamed worker put it there well over a hundred years ago, not ever imagining that someone would be appreciating it during the last part of the next century.

Forgetting about his initial embarrassment, he began to call for help. His voice sounded strange to him, as if it belonged to someone else. Remembering that the tractor was still running, he began to call out louder and louder. His voice sounded very loud from inside the well, but he suspected that it might sound distant and weak to anyone outside the well. He was getting colder and realized that he was unaware of how much time had passed. He tried to think about what time he would have fallen in and what time it now was. Had he been in the well ten minutes? Twenty minutes? The more he thought about it, the more confused he became. He was stuck in a point in time, just shivering in a well, holding on to the edge of a brick.

He wondered if his mother could hear the tractor running from the kitchen window, wondered if she was setting the table by now, and wondered if she had put the green onions in a glass of water on the table. Maybe she would hop in the car and drive over to check on him. Maybe she would call his sister's husband and ask him to go and check. Maybe a neighbor would be coming home from work and see the unoccupied tractor running and pull in to find out why.

He had been leaning his head against the side of the well, arms tucked closely to his chest, fingers still clinging to the brick. But now he looked up and decided it was time to try to reach the board again. This time, Aiden wedged his feet against each side of the well and tried to raise his body a few inches. But each time he tried, one foot or the other would slip down on the wet bricks. Then he tried twice more to elevate his body upward by kicking as hard as he could, but this time, he could not touch the board at all.

His fingers were getting tired and numb, and the joints of his fingers were aching. He wondered how long he could hold on. Was this how his life would end? That was all? Just like that? He could feel his feet, but they felt clumsy, like heavy blocks of wood were tied to his legs.

Again he wondered how long he had been in the well. The round patch of sky above looked darker and dimmer than it had before. It seemed like he'd been in there a long time now. Was that the tractor still running, or was he just hearing wind or a train somewhere?

Everything was becoming blurry and obscure. He was exhausted, drifting, random thoughts entering his mind and then departing quickly before he could hang on to them, distant and unfocused, floating away. He was very tired and very sleepy. If he could just go to sleep, every-thing would be fine. His fingers slowly began to slip away from the brick, but that was okay. The water was no longer cold. Sleep was never going to feel so good.

CHAPTER

8

Squirrel Shooting

I FIRST READ WASHINGTON IRVING'S TALE of Rip Van Winkle when I was about fourteen, 142 years after he wrote it. I was stirred by his flair for descriptive style and his ability to transport my mind to New York's Catskill Mountains. He described Rip as a man who would have "whistled life away in perfect contentment" if not for a nagging wife. He would temporarily put matrimony aside to go "squirrel shooting." At the age of fourteen, having just taken up that sport myself, I understood completely that shooting squirrels was only a small part of the soul-satisfying peace that results from spending the day surrounded by the beautiful solitude of the deep woods.

Before being old enough to hunt, I watched my dad and grandfather spend most of their spare time in late August and September involved in squirrel hunting. They left well before dawn, traveled to some mysterious destination, and returned four or five hours later in a good mood and full of stories about the details of the morning's hunt.

About the age of eleven or twelve, I thought I was old enough to go along, but I was not allowed to go until I was two years older. That year, I purchased a used Winchester Model 37 single shot 12-gauge shotgun for fifteen dollars and was at last able to go and help bring home some "timber chicken."

On weekends I could go with Dad on his days off. During the week, I could go alone by riding my bicycle out of town to the wooded bottoms along Fox Creek, which stretches from one end of the county to the other. In those days, it was not unusual to see a boy riding down the streets of a small town with a rifle or shotgun over his shoulder, a scene that might cause concern today.

I don't know if my strong attraction for the woods came about because of many subsequent years of "squirrel shooting" or if my love of the woods explains why I enjoy squirrel hunting. I suspect that the latter is the case because I have a good day even if I don't bring in any bounty.

Hunting squirrels is most productive early in the morning, and the woods are very different right before sunrise than at noon. Upon entering, you notice how cool the air is, even during warm weather. The damp, rich smell of the forest floor dwells in the air, and the dense canopy of branches and leaves hide the view of the purple and pink eastern sky as dawn nears. Trees are dark silhouettes of black that blend together, and at a distance of only a few yards, they cannot be differentiated from one another.

Even a familiar woods appears odd, eerie, and foreboding, and entering into dark, old growth timber with hundred-year-old trees towering above you can be disorienting. The occasional scurry of nocturnal residents can be heard and, if you are very quiet, you can sometimes hear the flapping of an owl's wings overhead as it searches for one last morsel on the blanket of leaves before it finds a favorite daytime perch. For a while, time stands still in the pre-dawn minutes, and you are strongly aware of the solitude, a feeling that can be a little disturbing and deliciously addictive at the same time.

Many years have gone by since the woods and I became such good friends. Unlike Rip, I have never met a band of peculiarly dressed, short, stocky fellows playing ninepin in the hollow of the deep woods, let alone stocky fellows with strong rum to quaff. That is not to say, however, that I have not been lost in some large tract of unfamiliar timber, wondering which way to turn, or that I have not experienced some uneasy times myself. One particular event comes to mind.

One hot day in early September, I lost John William Burns, Attorney at Law, up in Sangamon County. John was chief legal counsel for an organization that specialized in labor contract disputes. We had gotten to know each other fairly well because he or his staff had handled several arbitration cases for the department in which I worked.

John had grown up pheasant hunting in another state and suggested that he and I schedule a squirrel hunt together. While squirrel hunting is primarily a solitary sport, it can be enjoyed with another person if the forest is large enough to allow each hunter enough space to move around without the likelihood of bumping into the other. I knew of such a spot not far from town, so we agreed to go on a Saturday morning.

I picked up John at his house well before daylight, and we drove to an area west of Springfield that belonged to a friend. During the drive, we chatted about guns, shells, and squirrel hunting techniques until arriving at our destination. I parked along the side of the road near a large culvert that went under the road and drained water from a small stream at a low point on the property.

Here we had a discussion about how we would each proceed. The forest was rectangular in shape with the longest part running east and west. The north and south edges were bordered by fields that were mostly overgrown with brush. The east side was a more open field, extending a few miles toward town, and it was partly farm ground. The west outskirts of the city were marked by a bustling four-lane highway some distance away.

It was agreed that John would hunt east on the north side of the woods and I would hunt east on the south side of the woods. Upon reaching the far side of the woods, we would each turn toward the middle and meet to measure our success. If we missed each other in the woods, we would meet at the car at around 9:30 a.m.

It was a warm, humid morning, which is normally not good for hunting because the squirrels are not as active. I moved slowly through the woods, knowing that it would take John longer to find his way east because the forest was less open and unfamiliar to him. I gradually made my way to the far side, which was marked by an old fence line. As agreed, I then turned toward the center of the area to meet John. I had only seen a couple of squirrels on my walk and had only shot one of those. I had heard John shoot once too.

Not seeing my companion, I found a comfortable place to sit and wait, thinking he had not yet arrived at the meeting spot. After about forty minutes, I decided to proceed down the opposite side, hoping that I would see him along the way. Seeing nothing, I arrived back at the car at 9:30 a.m., fully expecting to see him there. He was nowhere in sight.

I found a shady place and waited for almost an hour. Twice during that time I made a loud noise by repeatedly striking the drainage culvert with a piece of concrete I had found, thinking he might be guided by the sound. By then it was getting quite hot, probably somewhere in the nineties, and the air was still and muggy.

I put my shotgun away in the car and decided to go out and search. Perhaps he had sat down and fallen asleep, or maybe he was waiting out a crafty squirrel hiding behind a large oak limb. It occurred to me that he could even have developed chest pains and collapsed in the woods. The thought of that made me duly concerned.

I moved back and forth through the woods looking for him, at first slowly and quietly. But as time went on and there was no sign of him, I picked up my pace. I whistled and shouted his name many times but heard no response. I couldn't imagine where he could be and became increasingly worried. I had no doubts that he would have heard me and called back if he were able to, so I began to fear the worst.

With perspiration streaming down my face, I returned to the car and wondered if I should go to the nearest house and call the police. Most of all, I wondered what John's wife, Lorraine, would be thinking by now. Surely she must be wondering why he wasn't home yet.

It was now 11:00 a.m., an hour and a half after the time we were to meet. I decided that there was no point in waiting any longer and decided to go home. Once there, I would start calling people, with Lorraine first on the list.

I drove the short distance home with a dozen scenarios racing through my mind. I didn't even bother to pull into the garage when I got home, I just left the car in the drive and rushed into the house. My wife came out of the kitchen with a concerned look on her face.

"Where have you been? I was getting worried about you. Is everything okay?" she asked.

"I lost John Burns," I replied. "We were supposed to meet at the car, but he never showed up. I have no idea where he is."

"Well, call his wife right away. She has already called twice asking if you were home yet, and I told her you never stay out this long."

As I dialed the phone, dread and fear again encompassed me. What should I say? Should I ask if he had an undisclosed heart condition or would that make matters worse? Would she be upset that I left him there? Should I have searched more?

By then the phone was ringing, and Lorraine came on the line.

I identified myself and asked if she had heard from John.

"Sure," she replied. "He's right here. Do you want to talk to him?"

I was stunned. "What?"

"Here he is," she said.

"Gary, this is John," said my morning's companion in the same slow, calm voice he would have used if I had called his office to inquire about a case.

"Hi, John. Where have you been and how did you get home?" I asked with great interest.

"Oh, Lorraine gave me a ride," was the matter-of-fact response.

I could think of little to say in response. "Oh, I see." I wondered how he had managed to contact her. "Did you walk out of the woods and go to a nearby house?" I asked. Not only was this in the days before cell phones, it was at a time and in a place where someone coming to your door asking to use your phone did not immediately scare the bejesus out of you and prompt an immediate call to the local police.

"No, I called from the shopping mall in town," he said.

John had been a lawyer for a long time and had asked plenty of logical, sequential questions to gather facts, so he realized that he was not going to get off the witness stand until the full story had been told. He began to elaborate.

"Well," he chuckled, "I got lost out there I guess. I got so turned around that I didn't know which way the car was, so I just kept walking. I got to where I could hear cars off in the distance and eventually came to Veterans Parkway. From there, I could see the big shopping mall, so I crossed the parking lot, went into Macy's, and found a phone to call Lorraine. Then she drove in and picked me up."

I realized that what he had done was one long walk on a hot day. And he was wearing a hunting coat. Then I envisioned him walking along one of the busiest streets in town carrying a shotgun and wondered about the dozens of people who must have seen him. "You . . . you . . . carried your shotgun into the mall?" I asked.

"Oh, no," he replied. "I hid it in the weeds along the highway. Then, after Lorraine came and got me, we pulled off the road and picked it up."

There wasn't much to say after that. I was relieved that John was safely home, but I was also feeling a little miffed that he had been having a cool drink in his favorite chair while I was worriedly searching the hot woods, knee-deep in poison ivy.

There had been no soul-satisfying peace in the woods that day, and I'd bagged but one squirrel. Unlike Rip, who'd at least had a nice sleep in a green knoll, I had spent my time trudging through the woods on a hot day. And to no avail.

John and I never again slipped off together into the woods to engage in the sport of squirrel shooting. I don't think he asked, and I don't think I offered.

I didn't stop squirrel hunting, though. Just like Rip Van Winkle, I occasionally took a stroll in the woods to gather in some peace apart from the clamor of the world. When I got lost in the timber for a spell, I only had myself to worry about. And I always managed to find my way out of the woods and back home again without the help of Macy's.

CHAPTER

9

The Cleveland Foundry Company Puritan Oil Heater

 WHETHER DONE WITH FOCUSED INTENTION, unthinking casualness, or complete innocence, some of the things we do in life will come back to haunt us in one way or another, sooner or later, and cause us to question ourselves. Few get a free lifetime pass as the ticktock of time counts out our days. The most visible indication of this, of course, is physical. Years of overeating and getting too little exercise will eventually cause problems. There is a good chance that smoking will too. Not so visible and more subtle are the memories of our relationships with those we care about and the questions about them that arise in our minds when enough time has passed to allow us to revisit those memories more impartially. Hopefully, we conclude that we did, in fact, do the right thing after all.

It was the day of my annual appointment with my dermatologist. Those long, sunny days of my youth appear to be at the root of such appointments, extending back to a time before the terms *sunblock* and *ozone layer* were taken seriously, back when a sunburn was of little consequence for all but the very fair of skin. Manly summer jobs outside working without a shirt and days off hanging out at the pool or beach were a part of growing up in a rural area. I can't change my youthful overexposure to the sun, so every year I see the skin doctor to determine if there is anything surfacing from my past.

My wife and I left for the doctor's office on one of those lovely late-fall mornings when the remaining leaves were falling quickly. The drive up Route 45 would take about an hour. Most of the crops had been harvested, and the sun streaked across the wheat stubble and what remained of cornstalks. It was a pleasure to see the open fields and freshly disked earth.

We drove through a hilly wooded area, appreciating what was left of the grand fall colors, and then entered an area of flat, open land, which provided long views of fields with farms tucked into groves of shade trees. On the east side of the highway, we noticed two small hand-printed signs where a road turned between two open fields. On one sign the words *garage sale* were printed, almost neatly, and the other homemade sign, with larger but more primitive and downward sloping letters, contained the single word *antiques*.

Having plenty of time before the appointment, being somewhat intrigued by the signs so many miles from a town, and feeling somewhat attracted to the mystery of what treasures might lie beyond, I made a quick signal for a right turn.

The narrow road was paved at first and barely wide enough for two cars. It was straight and inviting as it led through a large field, but it was also somewhat confusing because there was no house nearby on either side. We continued driving for about half a mile until the road intersected another small road running north and south. The road we were on continued east but turned into gravel and appeared to be more of a farm lane than a public road. We noticed another small hand-printed sign on a wooden fence post that beckoned us on.

After driving another couple of hundred yards or so, we saw a farmhouse in the distance at the end of the road. The house had been built on a small rise. It had a barn and a few weathered sheds in front of and on one side of the house. The large yard contained a few trees that appeared a little windswept, no doubt from many years of standing in the open with very little to block the wind.

As we pulled up to park between the house and sheds, I noticed an older man working some distance north of the house in what might have been an old orchard. Either he didn't notice the car pull up or did notice but was too busy at his task to care because he did not offer an acknowledging glance in our direction.

We got out of the car and saw that the large three-sided machine shed directly in front of the house contained rows of tables crowded with an assortment of items. Hearing the house front door open, we turned to see a person whose appearance was exactly what you might envision an old farm wife to look like. Beverly, as she later called herself, was tall and thin. She had thick hair that was mostly gray and unusually long for a woman of her age, extending well beyond her shoulders. An old shirt was covered with a waist-length cotton jacket, and her worn blue jeans and old leather boots appeared to have seen many seasons of work. Her rugged but alert face recorded the weathering of her life in an interesting way, not unlike the aged vertical wooden boards that protected the contents of the shed.

I greeted her as she was still exiting the front door, and she replied with a smile and a glib flow of observations that continued long after she crossed the porch, came down the stairs, and stood at our sides. I instantly liked her unassuming friendliness and energetic, joyful demeanor. Although she looked old, she moved quickly and easily, like someone much younger. She gave us a summary of the recent and predicted weather, her love of all things old, her lost hope of one day owning an antiques store, and a hint of her appreciation of a simple country life, all while the cool breeze blew her uncontrolled hair around and in front of her face.

Beverly explained that she had always liked to keep family heirlooms, large and small, and had many things that belonged to her parents, her husband's parents, and departed neighbors. She understood that she could not keep everything, but she had a hard time parting with anything.

Each item had a story and memory that were linked in her mind, so throwing out the item meant, in some way, throwing out the memory as well. But she knew she needed to part with at least some of what she'd been collecting for many years.

"Young folks today are not interested in old junk, so it makes no sense for me to pass these things on to family members. I might as well lighten the load by selling some of it," she said. She had started retrieving items from the house, basement, and out buildings and arranging them in some order to sell. "When I sell a few items and make room on a table, I drag out more stuff to take their place."

Glancing around as she spoke, I could see no order whatsoever to the items. Everything was so close together that it was difficult to focus on any one item. She said the items were grouped partly by the family member or friend who had once owned them and partly according to the price. The tables to the north side were the least expensive and the items gradually increased in value or price as one moved towards the south wall. Some items were priced, but most were not. Some had been reduced in price several times by placing a new piece of tape with a lower price over the old piece of tape with a higher price. The original item might have had $10.50 on the first piece of tape, then $7.00 and $4.50 on subsequent pieces.

The age of the items covered a period from the late 1800s up through approximately the 1950s, and they ranged from household items to old tools and farm supplies. She had a significant collection of salt and pepper shakers that had been owned by an aunt, depression glass that had come from her grandmother, a set of heavy glass water goblets that had gained a blue tint with age, and old medicine and whiskey bottles that came with corks or glass stoppers. Some things were collectible and might be seen in an antiques store and others seemed to have little or no value.

I tried to browse through the tables, realizing it might take two hours just to see everything that was there. Focusing was difficult because of the nonstop stories that flowed from Beverly's mouth about the pieces I noticed, including a good guess as to the age and use of the piece. I paused to examine an old Seth Thomas wall clock, and she explained that it had belonged to her husband's father. I checked to see if it worked. It didn't. Another story followed about how her husband could fix most anything on the farm.

I had a few quiet moments looking around when she noticed my wife showing interest in or being near a particular item that held yet another story she could relate about its trip through history. I smiled at the thought of how many long-departed souls must have owned and loved all these things, probably enough to double the size of a large family reunion.

I noticed a rather large, oddly shaped glass container with the words *The Cleveland Foundry Company* embossed on the side along with a triangular design. The thick, heavy glass had bubbles in it and a pockmark on the bottom where it had been formed, indicating that it was quite old. It had a narrow top that I noticed was the same size as the top of the fuel storage compartment of a kerosene lamp. I had collected old oil lamps for years and had never seen one of these. It was oozing with character and patina.

Beverly explained that it was from a home coal oil heater that was used to help heat homes in the late 1800s and early 1900s. She said she remembered how it con-nected to the heater her dad's uncle had owned and that it was now a rare item because being so large, it was easily bumped and broken. It was a great find and in very good condition with no cracks or chips. I held it to the light and could see that light blue tint. It was marked at $4.50, but before I could ask, she said that she would sell it for $3.50.

While I was looking at some antique oil lamps nearby, Beverly asked if I had seen the two large old wooden ammo boxes in the corner. The boxes were about three feet long, a foot deep, and maybe six inches high. On each end of each box was a heavy rope handle. She explained that they were US military ammunition boxes, probably once containing M-16 rifle shells. She had kept the boxes because of the stenciled wording on the outside of the box, which, among other things, had the date of October 1968 and the words *Viet Nam*.

"I have kept those boxes around here for years because they remind me of my brother," she said. "He was killed in Viet Nam the very next month after that date. I always thought I would make something out of them and did put shelves in one, as you can see. How much do you think I should sell them for, and what could be made from them?" she asked.

"Oh, I don't really know," I replied. "I have a couple of them at home in my shop that I store tools in under my workbench. About all of us growing up in that time period had a friend or family member who was killed over there I guess. Two guys from my high school class died there."

"My brother was younger than me, and I was already married when he left," she said. "He was drafted pretty soon after he was out of school, like they did back then. He went for his basic army training and returned home on leave for two weeks before he left. He told me that he'd had a dream that he was going to die in Viet Nam and didn't want to go. Do you think he really knew? Maybe a premonition? He wanted to borrow some money from me so he could escape and go to Canada. I thought about it and told him no. Dad was in World War II when he was that age. How could I tell Mom and Dad that I had loaned him money to go to Canada?"

The tone of Beverly's voice had changed, and she spoke more slowly as she told this story. I looked down at the ammo boxes, mostly to avoid looking into her eyes, wondering if she was going to ask me if she had done the right thing forty-seven years ago and hoping she wouldn't ask. She didn't.

"His girlfriend was pregnant then too, and he wanted to get married but didn't. He was almost done with his one year over there—only two weeks left I think—when he was killed by a Gook booby trap explosion. My folks didn't know for several days. His girlfriend decided she didn't want to keep the baby, so my husband and I agreed to take him and raise him. We didn't learn until after he was grown that we could have drawn Social Security to help raise him. Nobody ever told us that."

I looked around several minutes longer, pondering her words and wishing I had more time to look at the curious assortment of old things. I listened to a couple more of Beverly's stories when an item reminded her of how it came to be there. Finally, my wife pointed out that we needed to get going to be on time for my appointment.

Beverly returned to the house and came back with a notebook and a small cash box. She added up our purchases using a pencil, writing down a column of large numbers and then adding by hand. We paid her for an oil lamp that I wanted to add to my collection, a dish that my wife liked, and the very cool Cleveland Foundry Company Puritan Oil Heater oil container.

Beverly gave us her phone number and e-mail address so we could call her and look some more if we were driving by again.

We drove down the long lane through the field and back to the highway.

That night, as I admired my new pieces, I kept thinking about Beverly's stories, especially the one about her brother asking to borrow money. It occurred to me that though she was a strong woman, she must have questioned herself many times throughout her life, wondering if she had done the right thing by saying no to her brother's request, regardless of her good intentions. Was she now at peace with herself like we all hope to be in later life? Was that why she was now able to let the ammo boxes go and maybe the self-doubt as well? I hoped it was.

I used soapy water to wash away the years of dirt from the large, heavy glass lamp oil tank with the slight blue tint and was pleased that it came out bright and clear. I added a wick, brass lamp top, and globe, and placed it on an antique table where, when a visitor shows an interest, I can now add my own story and memory of its history to that of Beverly's.

Not all of us have nostalgic connections to material things, but most of us have unresolved memories, whether we realize it or not. Who hasn't awoken from a vivid dream at three o'clock in the morning and stared at the ceiling while pondering something from the past? Who hasn't found an old photograph or heard a song that reminds them of something they wish they had—or had not—said or done. As we journey in time, it might be good that we are reminded of uncertainties. It might also be good to keep those reminders close, so that when it is time to take that long, straight road between fields to our final destination, we can do so in peace.

CHAPTER

10

Sampson

THOSE LIVING IN A CITY might not realize that one of the best parts about living in the country is the variety of smells that drift around in the air. The blending of these scents can be confusing to the unacquainted, either man or beast, until they are sorted out. That takes concentration and practice. It is much like listening to instrumental music, which at first is just an enjoyable combination of sounds that may stimulate a mood, bring back memories, create energy, or help you relax. But by listening carefully, the sound of each instrument can be heard and appreciated individually for its own distinct contribution to the total.

Paying attention to the components of country smells was something Sampson had fine- tuned. Smells varied by the season, time of day, and direction of the wind. Morning smells were the most interesting to Sampson as he rested on his favorite spot on the back deck, and he would smell a combination of odors pulled from the ground and pond by the cooler temperatures of the previous evening. He enjoyed the smell of the trees, fields, and grass that floated along on the first breeze. Even the direction of the breeze changed the olfactory selections.

It had been a long, hot summer, and Sampson was glad it was over. His black coat soaked up the hot sun, though he could find temporary relief by following the shade of the many trees in the backyard. He would hollow out a spot close to the trunk of a large hickory tree, spin around a couple of times, and plop down with a thud, with little energy left to do more than look around in between naps. Sometimes he rested his handsome snout on the bare, dusty earth or over a tree root so he could see out a little farther in case anything moved, which wasn't often, except for the swaying of the trees or an occasional bird. His eyes would close slowly to the half-shut position, and his breathing would become slow and regular. At some point later—he never knew exactly when—he would begin to feel the warm sun, requiring him to move to a more shaded spot.

But with the evenings now cooler, Sampson awoke on this day near the foundation of the house with his rump and lower back pushed against the cool concrete. The cooler night had left more scents on the ground, and he resisted the temptation to jump up and sniff out any sign of nocturnal visitors. Instead, he lay silently and motionless as a "squirrel-get'im" carried a nut down the trunk of a shagbark hickory and nervously moved about with little spurts of motion that Sampson always found exciting.

When Sampson first came to John and Barb's house and John spotted a *squirrel-get'im* before Sampson noticed it, John always raised his arm, lowered his voice, and said, "Squirrel! Get'im!"

As Sampson grew larger and older, he learned that *squirrel-get'ims* could often be seen in the backyard. Sometimes two or three of them moved together in the yard, and sometimes one came close from the woods behind the house.

One morning, Sampson had been lying on the ground against the big hickory tree when two *squirrel-get'ims* chased each other noisily down the tree trunk until they were almost to the ground, barely above his back. The lowest *squirrel-get'im* whipped around the trunk in one last circle, dragging his bushy tail across Sampson's unnoticed nose. Sampson had been startled, but recovered just in time to lunge up at the *squirrel-get'im*, unfortunately missing his mark. Sampson had tried to race *squirrel-get'ims* across the yard many times, but he had never beaten one to a tree or even gotten very close to one.

Now, as Sampson lay by the foundation of the house, a *squirrel-get'im* relaxed and hesitated as he hopped over a branch lying on the ground. Sampson focused intently, tensed his muscles, and felt the almost overwhelming sensation to lurch toward the squirrel well up inside of him, a sensation that often followed a shout of "Go!" from

John. He had learned that if he resisted the *Go!* for a while and remained motionless, the *squirrel-get'im* might get much closer. In the hot days of summer, it had been much easier to resist *Go!* In fact, some days the heat had taken so much energy from him that he resisted *Go!* altogether.

But on this morning, the night air lingered around him and his only awareness of anything was putting *Go!* and *squirrel-get'im* together. Sampson tensed his muscles and moved forward. His dark eyes were motionless and intently focused, and in the next movement, he exploded forward with great energy toward his target, which immediately leaped up and ran toward the hickory.

Sampson was unaware of his paws digging into the earth as he propelled forward, kicking up little puffs of dust. He was unaware of anything except the distance between his eyes and the *squirrel-get'im*. And just when it appeared that he might at last snatch the *squirrel-get'im* from a lower tree limb, the *squirrel-get'im* sprang up the trunk, ascending beyond his reach.

Sampson placed his paws on the side of the tree trunk and peered upward, but the moment had passed. He barked a warning to the creature, which turned back around and hung upside down to look at him. Then it perched on a lower branch and looked nervously down at him, barking in a scornful, low tone.

As his interest faded, Sampson heard the back door open and saw John walk over to the bench, coffee in one hand and cigarette in the other. Sampson's tail wagged instantly and joy replaced *squirrel-get'im* completely. He trotted over to the deck, hopped up the familiar steps, and reached John as he sat down.

"Hey, Sampson," John said affectionately, rubbing the back of Sampson's neck.

Sampson sniffed John's hand, and when he didn't smell the scent of *biscuit,* he sat down within John's reach, letting joy linger in his being.

John was the primary attraction from inside the house, with *eat* and *biscuit* being close seconds. Sometimes John had *eat* or *biscuit* with him, the very best combination of good things. But today, there was no scent of either nearby.

John was Sampson's best friend and companion. He loved John. If John went anywhere outside the house, Sampson always followed to see what John was going to do. Sometimes John drove the tractor down a trail in the woods and stopped to split firewood, an activity Sampson didn't care for because it was noisy and boring. But other times, John just walked through the woods and along the country fields, which was much more fun.

Sampson always ran ahead of John and stopped suddenly when he came across an interesting scent. Then he identified and catalogued the scent in his mind. Most of the time, the scent was familiar, but once in a while it was new and warranted more attention. If John stopped to sit on a log, Sampson stopped too, stretching out in the leaves and waiting for a *squirrel-get'im* to move.

One common scent was of the big dogs John called *deer.* In the early morning, their scents were everywhere:

in the fields, along the lane, around the pond, and sometimes even in the yard around the house, especially near the flower beds. These strange, large creatures fascinated Sampson because he could never quite figure them out. They seemed to be big dogs, but they did not have an interest in him or in joining his pack. Standing at a safe distance, they stared at him, motionless, for several minutes. Rarely would they notice a *squirrel-get'im*, but even when they did, they never chased or caught one. They had gotten used to him and seemed to have little fear as long as he stayed in the yard by the house.

Sampson respected these creatures and sensed a feeling of respect for him from them. Occasionally, he followed their scent through the woods just to see where they were going. He had no idea what they liked to eat, but they seemed to spend hours munching on something in the fields, as if *biscuits* were lying about, but Sampson could not confirm this. He admired their free spirit. They seemed to come and go as they pleased.

In the more than two years he'd been with John and Barb, Sampson had never worried about getting enough to eat. *Eat* was always there, usually in a bowl on the covered deck. During the coldest part of winter, Sampson could come inside where it was warm and where there was plenty of *eat*, and sometimes John or Barb even shared some of their own *eat* with him. Sampson was only allowed to stay in the laundry room, and although the laundry room door was always open, he was subject to the honor system and not allowed to wander around the house. He didn't think John and Barb knew, but the lure of the living room woodstove was sometimes too great. He would wait until all was quiet in the house and venture there to bask in the glow of the steady heat, then return to the laundry room at the first hint of the sounds that meant John or Barb might appear.

As the nights got cooler, Sampson did less sleeping and felt more energetic. He roamed around the fields and woods until late at night, sensing that other creatures were wandering more too. Smells became more frequent and stronger. Sounds were magnified by the drying leaves beginning to fall and cover the ground. It was during these times that Sampson felt a need for the freedom of more solitary exploration and less need for his pack members, John and Barb. His sense of dependence lessened and the exhilaration of being on his own increased.

As fall turned into early winter, the ground began to frost over at night. Sampson began sleeping on the porch or under the awning, beneath the tractor. He never really got cold because his coat was becoming thicker and bushier.

John didn't leave the house as often now, but he and Sampson still liked spending time together when he did. Almost always, John had *biscuit* in his hand or pocket and tossed one to him. He had learned to catch it before it hit the ground. Barb only came outside on warm afternoons and sometimes called his name in a friendly tone.

Following one particularly cold night, Sampson began to hear a distant noise that was unusual. Loud booms started at daylight and echoed through the woods. Sampson didn't know what it meant and didn't really like the sound of it, although he had a distant memory of something like this happening before. He held his nose high in the air and sniffed in all directions, but he could not detect anything abnormal. Sometimes the loud booms sounded close, and sometimes they sounded very far away.

As the sunlight began to filter through the trees in the backyard, John came out on the deck carrying his long gun. Sampson had seen the gun many times and always got a little excited when he saw it, mostly because it meant he and John would walk together in the woods. When John raised the gun quickly, Sampson immediately raised his head and looked around because that motion was often followed by a loud noise. And when that happened, a *squirrel-get'im* would often jump to the ground and lie motionless. Sampson would run over to it, pick it up, and bring it back to John. Sampson wanted to keep the *squirrel-get'ims*, but he understood that they belonged to John. Twice last winter, John had pointed the gun above the pond and large birds splashed into the water. With a little coaxing, Sampson had jumped into the cold water, swam out to get them, and brought them back to John.

But this morning, John didn't leave the deck. He just sat down in his chair. Sampson sat down beside him at first and then lay down as he felt the sun getting warmer on his side. Suddenly, half asleep, Sampson leaped into the air when he heard the sound of the gun. He quickly looked all around but didn't see any movement at first. Then he cocked his head as he heard loud rustling of the leaves just inside the woods.

John quickly got up and walked toward the sound, and Sampson raced ahead, arriving first at the source of it. There, lying motionless on the ground, was one of the big dogs John called *deer*. Its strong scent was everywhere, stronger than Sampson had ever noticed before. He instinctively looked at its head and into its large, brown eyes, which did not look back at him. Sampson looked excitedly at John, who was still looking at the *deer* and lighting a cigarette. Sampson felt very confused about what had just happened, but he never doubted that John, as the leader of the pack, always knew what to do.

John took a knife from his belt and began to cut into the animal. Sampson watched intently, barely moving as John worked. The innards were removed and placed below and beside the big dog called *deer*. Sampson's senses were keen and fully encompassed by the event. These were scents he had no experience with, and they confused him greatly, making him feel uneasy. There was something that felt wrong about it.

Once complete, John drove his truck to the creature, pulled it into the truck bed, and drove to a nearby tree, where he hung the creature by its hind legs from a stout tree limb.

After John picked up his gun and returned to the house, Sampson returned to where the creature had been and sat for a long time. He didn't really know what had happened, but something about it made him very uncomfortable. The big dog called *deer* had fallen to the ground after the same kind of sound that had always done the same thing to *squirrel-get'im*. John, the leader of his pack, had something to do with it, but Sampson wasn't quite sure what his part in it had been. Whatever it was, he didn't like it, and he began to have doubts about his pack leader. He sat near the tree where the creature was hanging and watched it for a long time before returning to the deck where John had been sitting. Later, John came out with a shovel and buried the gut pile at the edge of the woods while Sampson watched from afar. Several times that night, Sampson approached the hanging creature and sniffed the scent, still confused about the meaning of the event.

When John came out the next morning, coffee in hand, Sampson did not come to him as usual. He sat and watched John for a few minutes and then curled up to nap. Soon after, Sampson felt like heading off to be alone, so he walked far into the woods and across the next field, a place where he had not been before. Something in him was stirred, and he kept walking for days. He found what food he could as he made his journey with no destination.

Several days passed, and John and Barb searched many hours for Sampson. They scoured the fields and woods near their property and called neighbors to see if Sampson had been seen. They drove around the township roads and lanes, stopping once in a while to honk the truck horn. Sampson's disappearance remained a mystery to them.

Two weeks later, John was working on his tractor when he saw something move by the pond. When he recognized it, he called out to Barb, who was in the house. "Hey, Sampson is home!"

As Barb came onto the porch, Sampson walked into the yard wagging his tail enthusiastically. John sat on the ground and began petting Sampson's head. "Where in the world have you been, ole boy?" he asked, repeating himself several times.

Barb invited Sampson into the house and opened a can of *eat* that was usually brought out only on special occasions. John and Barb said his name many times and rubbed his neck and back.

That night, Sampson was allowed to sleep in the laundry room, and he again went to the woodstove and basked in its warmth after the house became quiet.

When morning came, John got his coffee and went out to the deck to smoke. Sampson followed him out and briefly sat down next to him, happy that John had *biscuit* in his coat pocket.

Sampson sat quietly and gazed at the field. But before John could finish his coffee, Sampson walked down the steps, across the yard, and into the field, clearly focused on something. John watched from the deck. Finally, Sampson stopped in the field, turned around, and stood motionless, staring back at John. John and Sampson were too far away from one another to see each other clearly, but each felt the other's eyes.

And then Sampson turned away and continued to walk into the woods without looking back, never to return.

CHAPTER

11

The Thoughts of an Old Man

 ALWAYS HAVING THOUGHT OF HIMSELF as a practical and realistic fellow with a good dose of common sense, Fred Herrin had been rather surprised with himself over the last few weeks. He had never been one to mull over what might have been or compare himself and the way he lived to anyone or anything else. For most of his seventy-four years, he had been perfectly content to just lead a simple life with little concern about wealth or materialism. But now he found himself thinking about things.

Maybe it had something to do with age, he thought. Maybe it was natural and predictable for his thoughts to turn towards the past when there was more past in his life than there would be future. Maybe it was an unconscious game that his mind had initiated, triggered by the growing number of little aches and pains in his body. Or maybe it was a gradual dawning in his mind that several of his friends were not around anymore and that in a few years, he wouldn't be either. Although surprised to find himself with a philosophical side at all, it was a little entertaining to think beyond what he had in the house for lunch or wonder whether or not the newspaper boy would be late with the paper again.

Born in 1894 in the same house in which he now lived alone, Fred was about as happy and content as anyone could hope to be. The house had belonged to his parents. Along with his two brothers and four sisters, Fred had been raised there. The one-story clapboard frame house, which stood on the corner of Elm and Wilson Streets, was the only survivor on the block from the last century.

A large, old catalpa tree stood on the east side of the house and drowsily leaned at such an angle as to present a tempting challenge for the neighborhood kids to climb. Its large, thick, deep-green leaves shaded most of the east side of the house until almost noon, making it a welcome canopy on hot summer days. The old tree produced long seedpods that everyone had always called catalpa beans as summer progressed. Fred could recall his father, John, planting the tree, which he'd found growing as a sprout in the big vegetable garden behind the house. But he couldn't remember the year, though he knew it was sometime before World War I.

Two box elder trees grew in front of the house between the street and sidewalk. They provided a good place for English sparrows to roost at night. The only other tree in the yard was behind the house at the west corner of the dog park. It was a favored place for him to sit on hot days and talk to visitors.

Except for an old coal shed, the remainder of the deep lot was open and had been the site of a large vegetable garden most years since Fred was a boy. In recent years, Fred had only grown potatoes and sold them to Taylor's Market, the neighborhood grocery store across the street.

Between the back of the garden and the alley was a strip of grass several feet wide. Although there were no markers, this area was the resting place of several beloved dogs, some of which had slumbered there for close to sixty years. An old man misses many dogs, and Fred often thought about old Nip, or Lady, or Snowball as he passed by, recalling their companionship and the puppy teeth marks that could still be seen on the front leg of his mother's old pie safe, which still stood in the kitchen.

The inside of the house had not changed significantly since Fred was born there. At some point, the potbelly coal stove that had stood in the center of the living room had been replaced by a Warm Morning gas heater. Several layers of wallpaper and linoleum still covered the walls and floors. The kitchen had a door to the back porch and a window to the west, next to the kitchen stove, which was fueled by a hundred-gallon propane tank that sat outside the house.

A round wooden table with many coats of white paint was in one corner of the kitchen, and the antique pie safe stood on the east wall. Because the kitchen had been added on to the original part of the house at some point, it was a short step up into the living room where Fred spent most of his winter evenings. The davenport sat along one wall with an old stuffed chair, and a wooden rocking chair, once used by Fred's mother, sat near the space heater.

Everything in the house was old and had at some un-noticed point in history slipped beyond the classification of old-fashioned to that of antique. But Fred had never given a thought to such distinctions.

The house had no running water or electricity, but Fred had never had those things, so he didn't miss them. A well was located just outside the back door, and Fred used a metal pail to carry water inside to be heated for washing dishes or taking a bath. Several coal oil lamps lo-cated about the house were lit each evening. Most were plain looking, but the one on the kitchen table was painted. It had been his mother's favorite.

Fred had worked at a variety of jobs during his younger years, being content with whatever work he could get. He had been drafted into the army soon after the Great War broke out and had spent several months in Eu-rope. He'd taken part in the Meuse-Argonne Offensive in France as well as the Battle of the Somme. He was sitting in a muddy trench holding a Winchester Model 1897 trench gun when Armistice was declared.

Being the easygoing sort, he didn't give his military service much regard but did enjoy telling stories of his ex-periences during rugged, trench combat and everyday army life. His role as a character in his stories was always presented modestly, as if some current issue had merely reminded him of a long-ago connection. He would jokingly say that his war record read that he had great endurance and staying power.

Having never married, Fred returned to his parents' house after the war and spent much of his time working on construction projects through the 1920s and 1930s. During a great deal of that period, Fred worked for a concrete company that did much of the concrete work for the city and county, including the dam at the city pumping station on Fox Creek. When neighborhood boys asked him why he never got married, he replied that he'd never found anyone who would have him.

Being forty-five years old at the beginning of World War II, he had not been called to service. And there were plenty of jobs around while the younger men were gone. As his parents aged, they became more dependent on his help. His mother died in 1941, and he was left to care for his father, who passed away in 1949. By then, Fred was fifty-six years old. He inherited the old house.

Although his financial means were pretty modest, he was in good physical shape and didn't need or want much. He had several friends around town he enjoyed visiting with and a couple of loyal dogs for company. He read, listened to baseball games, and kept up on world events—an interest that had been developed thanks to his time overseas.

It was a mystery to Fred why his mind kept interrupting his daily routine. Bygones were just bygones, he thought.

*I'm happy to be alive and well, and I've had a life just as good
as anyone else's. All I need is just today, and the tomorrows will
string out in front of me and take care of themselves.* If there
had been a woman in his life, she would have been old by
then, just like him, and he supposed she would be telling
him what to do. He was happy with the way things were
and decided to go fishing the next day.

The sun seemed to warm the air early the next morning. It was almost hot for a day late in September, as if
summer was tugging on fall's pant leg as it quickened its
pace towards frosty October nights. Fred had risen before
dawn, as usual, and heated up some water for a cup of
Sanka. The breakfast dishes had already been washed as
the pink and lavender eastern sky melted into sunrise.
There was something very hopeful about each new morning, he thought, even if he was old. He placed a sandwich
in an empty bread wrapper, folded it several times, and put
it in a canvas shoulder bag, along with a quart jar of water.

By 6:45, he was walking down the street to the west
edge of the small town, and by 7:30 he baited his first hook
at the creek's edge. Even his hip pain, which had grown
from a minor irritation a few years back to a predictable
burdensome ailment, had been barely noticeable this
morning and demanded only a couple of rests during the
walk from town. In fact, it had occurred to him that perhaps it was not his hip at all that compelled him to stop
and lean against that white oak tree. It was just a good spot
to pause and survey the creek bottoms as he stepped off the
farming road and followed the fencerow to the slough.

Anyway, wasn't it about time for a fellow to slow down and appreciate the walk as well as the fishing, not because he must, but because the haste of his youth, with its shallow concerns, had given way to a lifetime of memories? At some point, he thought, impulsive actions ought to be replaced with reflective analysis and little indecisions replaced with contentment. Weren't old age and physical limitations just nature's way of ensuring that life is seen from all perspectives rather than just one, and an inexperienced one at that?

The day was turning out to be a good one for an old man. The morning had passed quickly, filled with the immediate details of fishing. At noon, the browning grass along the field's edge seemed to produce a sweet, dry smell as the sunlight beat down on its long, arching waves. Only three weeks earlier, it had been shaded by the elm trees that grew between the bean field and the hardwoods that marked the end of tillable land and the beginning of the creek bottoms.

Although he had fished up and down the bottoms since he was in grade school, this spot was his favorite. The creek here was straight for almost two blocks, which was inconsistent with its meandering nature. The banks were steep on both sides with only a few indentations permitting easy fishing. The water's depth ranged from four to nine feet, except during rainy or extremely dry periods. Even during a drought, when the water slowed to a standstill, a good, long pool of water remained.

The bank itself was closely lined with oak and hickory trees, some quite large, with their branches meeting in several places high above the center of the creek, providing bridges for squirrels desiring some nut or berry morsel on the opposite side. Years of spring rains had exposed many tree roots along and down the bank, providing handy footholds and handholds to climb down or up. The bank's east side was the edge of a long wooded area extending up and down the creek for several miles, interrupted only by an occasional gravel road. But the west side was bordered by a ribbon of trees seventy yards wide at this point and ending in a soybean field. Even on hot days, the air around the shady creek remained several degrees cooler than the field, and its coolness and shade were always an inviting end to the walk from town.

As far as he knew, no one besides him visited this place anymore. In years past, neighborhood boys accompanied him to the bottoms and spent the day with him. The boys had long since grown into adulthood, and the old man was now left to his own thoughts for companionship.

By noon he had caught five catfish, or yellow-bellies as he called them, which would mean a fine fish dinner sometime later. He had lifted the stringer out of the water to admire his catch after his simple but satisfying lunch. Later, when the fishing slowed down and drowsiness overcame him, he leaned back on the sandy bank, watched the branches moving in the breeze, and fell sound asleep.

Awakened by a quickening of the breeze and a slight chill developing in the air, the old man had taken a walk up the creek to examine whatever might catch his attention and then returned, mildly bothered to discover that during his absence, fish had stolen the bait from one line.

By 3:45, without the addition of any more fish to his catch, Fred decided to strike off for home. He finished bundling his poles together with two old leather dog collars, balanced them on his right shoulder, pulled the fish from the water, and followed the creek to where it was nearest the field.

As he emerged into the field's first row, his foot caught in some tall, thickly matted grass that made him lose his balance. At the same instant, his lurch made the end of the fishing poles thrust upward into low-hanging branches of the undergrowth. The result pitched the old man forward in a twisting, falling motion that culminated in a rather hard, uncontrolled landing, with poles, fish, and shoulder bag all clattering down around him. His hip joint, thinking it had given up such contortions forty years earlier, voiced its objection by being the center of a raw pain that went up his side and down his leg.

Immediately angered by the fall and pain and determined to fight back, the old man jerked his leg upward to free it from the grass. But that only caused a second round of protest from his worn hip. Partly in response to the pain and partly not knowing what his next move should be, he let his body go limp. The pain subsided at once, and he found himself staring up at the blue, cloudless September sky. A smile— almost a grin—came across his face as he thought how silly he must look with his wrinkled body lying half in the bean field and half in the undergrowth, surrounded by fish and gear, as if he had intentionally and carelessly rid himself of such burdens and flung himself down for another nap.

He thought of himself in his youth and how his strong legs, like iron beams, would have crashed through such a trivial obstacle, barely noticing it at all. For a moment longer, he turned to gaze at the soybean plant closest to his head and studied the dry bean pods gently moving in the warm sun. Then he rolled onto his stomach, pulled himself to his knees, placed a weathered, age-spotted hand in the fork of a stout little tree, and pulled himself to his feet.

He laughed out loud at himself, at his passing anger, at his aging body, at age, and at time itself. Looks like all is as it should be really, he thought. Life is still good. Then he arranged his shoulder bag, picked up his poles and fish, smiled, and walked down the edge of the field to the slough and on toward home.

He would clean the fish and maybe fry up some of them for supper. There was nothing like freshly caught fish, and there was no reason to defer the meal. And assuming he would see another sunrise, there would be some for breakfast too.

ACKNOWLEDGMENTS

I AM THANKFUL FOR the encouragement of friends and family while writing these stories. A special thanks to Carol Vaughn Shafer, my former high school classmate, for her enthusiastic encouragement. Much thanks, too, to my skillful editor, Melanie Mulhall, for her guidance. Also thanks to my talented designer, Bob Schram. I am especially grateful to my wife, Amber, for her patient suggestions and efforts, which were insightful at every turn.

ABOUT THE AUTHOR

GARY TOTTEN grew up in Richland County, in rural southeastern Illinois, and came to appreciate the friendliness, values, trials, humor, and pride of its hard-working people. After a professional career away from his hometown, he retired and returned to his roots. He now lives a quiet country life with his wife, Amber, and two dogs.